IN DUTCH AGAIN

An Amish Country Mystery

By

Barbara Workinger

This book is a work of fiction. Places, events, and situations in this story are purely fictional. Any resemblance to actual persons, living or dead, is coincidental.

ISBN: 1-4033-2430-1

Library of Congress Control Number: 2002091511

This book is printed on acid free paper.

Printed in the United States of America
Bloomington, IN

1st Books - rev. 07/22/02

Many people helped make this book possible. Thanks to my Amish friends, who know who they are, but would not wish to be singled out. Thanks to The Lancaster County Prison for the tour and advice on the Lancaster County criminal justice system.

Thank you, too to the great resources of Elizabethtown College; to The People's Place in Intercourse, Pennsylvania, both of whom helped me get the details correct and answered many questions.

I appreciate the line by line critiques of my friend and critique partner, Dr. David Shreiner and my agent and friend, Sara Camilli. Thanks to my daughter, Amy Kratz for her suggestions and support; to my kids, who always told me I could; my mother, Louise Glass and my late father, Reg Tibbetts who always told me I would.

Dedication

To Paul-with love

Author's Note;

Although I have tried to be accurate in my depiction of Lancaster County's Old Amish people, this is a work of fiction and I have taken liberties with the names and places in the county. Other than the names of well-known places, any similarities to real people or actual places or events is coincidental.

CHAPTER ONE

It was wedding weather in Amish country, crisp and exhilarating. There couldn't be a better place to live, Hannah Miller thought as she crunched through a pile of maple leaves as red as the glow on her cheeks. Almost November and time for winter, time for weddings, and as Hannah would soon find out, time for murder.

Hannah, called "Granny Hanny" by just about everyone in Lancaster County, was Amish, and a well-known quilt maker. Today she was on her way to deliver a quilt to her non-Amish neighbor, Annette Adams. Hannah knew Annette was anxious for it, and the day was so sparkling, that Hannah decided to walk the mile separating her family's dairy farm from the Adams property to deliver it in person. She had another happy errand at the Adams anyway, to deliver a wedding invitation; her grandson, Josh was marrying Susannah Schuler the first Wednesday in November. Tuesdays and Thursdays in November were the traditional times for Amish weddings, but this year a few were being held on Wednesdays. Harvest was over and the Amish families could celebrate. Thinking of the wedding made Hannah smile in happy anticipation. The family had been through some sticky times to get to it.

Annette's house sat on two acres of rich, loamy soil in the middle of what had once been a cornfield, and was now an empty, flat stretch of land looking curiously out of place, with only one huge maple tree and several dozen spindly, newly planted ones to keep it company. Although the house gave every appearance of "having some age," as an antique dealer like Annette would say, it was a new home, finished only the previous summer. A large Victorian style farmhouse, surrounded on all sides by deep, cool, shaded porches, Annette had filled the inside with costly, authentic antiques and wonderful art and crafts. Hannah knew some folks thought it strange Annette wouldn't spend the money to put in some big trees to match that lonely maple, for after all, she was a wealthy woman. But Annette's interest in the house stopped where the porch ended.

The house was Annette's territory, and the yard, had been her husband Bob's. An empty hole, destined for a swimming pool, and a half finished pool house remained as Bob had left them when he walked out of Annette's life, and apparently off the planet, three months ago.

Hannah had known Annette, or Nettie, as she was nicknamed since she was a little girl (and one of Doc Hope's identical twin daughters.) The twins, Nettie and Jennet, spent most of their childhood trying to fool people into thinking each was the other. Hannah could usually tell them apart. Annette was temperamental and usually into trouble while Jennet, or Jen as she was called, was sweet natured and always perfectly behaved. They reminded Hannah of one of her favorite Amish quilts, "Sunshine and Shadows."

The grown up Nettie now owned a well-known antique store in Lancaster, and people traveled from all over the country to buy her early American and authentic Amish wares. She specialized in Amish quilts.

Jennet was now a renowned fashion commentator with a syndicated television show. She flew from one fashion capitol of the world to another interviewing the glamorous big names of haute couture. Being Amish, Hannah was amused at how much attention the "English," the name Amish called anyone who wasn't Amish, paid to such stuff and nonsense. Still and all, Jennet made a good living from such silliness.

As Hannah approached the white painted steps of Annette's porch, she was surprised at the accumulation of debris on the normally pristine area. The wind had made a mess of the decorations. An ornamental scarecrow, carefully dressed in faded jeans and a plaid shirt had tipped over into the porch swing, looking for all the world like a drunk who didn't quite make it home. A carved jack-o-lantern had tumbled over, its candle lolling impudently through the smiling mouth. Leaves littered the steps and huddled against the house. Despite being "English", Nettie was normally as picky as any Amish housewife about her porch. This time of year it didn't take more than overnight for leaves to accumulate, and it was obvious to Hannah Nettie hadn't swept her porch that morning.

Hannah reached the front door and rang the bell. Silence was the only answer. Hannah rang again. The quilt, one of Hannah's handmade masterpieces, was made to order to Nettie's exacting specifications using more spools of thread than Hannah normally would, which insured more stitches to the inch and a heavily quilted piece. Hannah thought it was a beauty with a design of dozens of white snowflakes on a creamy white background. All white, and not light, Hannah thought, shifting the bulky bundle in her arms.

Nettie's car sat in the driveway. She must be home. Nettie knew Hannah would have the quilt ready anytime and told her she would be home all that day and the next. Unlike Hannah, Nettie wouldn't walk a block if she didn't have to. Besides, there was nowhere to go. Town was five miles away.

Hannah set the quilt, carefully wrapped in white paper and tied neatly with cord, on the only piece of furniture still left on the porch from summer, a swing, and walked around the porch, calling Nettie's name, then listening. The only sound was the drone of a small airplane high above in the cornflower blue sky.

One of Nettie's few reactions to her husband's disappearance was to install a high tech burglar alarm. Hannah had little idea how it operated except she knew it shrieked like a child with a nightmare, only louder, when it went off.

Hannah returned to the front door to try the bell once again. This time she pressed her finger to the bell and put her ear to the door. She heard the bell, and knew it worked. Once again there was no response from inside. Hannah was becoming increasingly worried about Nettie. What if she was ill, or had an accident? Hannah decided to examine the alarm.

Having entered several times with Nettie, Hannah remembered the control box, operated by a key, was out of sight behind a shutter. Easing it away from the porch wall, she saw the alarm box glowing green, indicating the system was not activated. So, now what? "Try the doors, of course," she muttered to herself, her voice echoing hollowly on the empty porch.

The front door was unlocked and she pushed it open, calling Nettie's name. This side of the house, away from the light and deeply shaded by the cavernous porch, was as black as a moonless night. As she stepped into darkness, the door swung shut behind her with a heavy thud. Hannah jumped. Though not easily frightened, the sudden change from bright sunlight to the dark house unnerved her. For the first time it occurred to her she could be in danger. What if someone besides Nettie was in the house? She wished she could be like Daisy, her calico cat, and fluff herself out. She would like to look a lot bigger than her five foot, 100 pound self. But if someone was in there, she reasoned, he'd have trouble seeing her in the near darkness, small as she was and dressed in her Amish costume of unrelieved black.

She stopped calling, but advanced carefully, taking small steps onto the floorboards of the deep entryway, reaching out to avoid bumping into anything. She tried to remember the location of the lights. She recalled a panel of switches was next to the stairs by the banister. Her eyes were becoming used to the dark. There was obviously no one lurking or they would have dispatched her by now.

The wall loomed darkly in front of her as she reached out, fumbling for the switches. Suddenly, she slipped on something. She reached out for the banister, but her feet continued to slide and she fell to the floor with a thud.

It only took a minute for her to realize she wasn't hurt and using the banister to steady herself, she pulled herself to her feet. Carefully, she edged towards the light switches, her feet slipping on what she realized was a wet, sticky floor. Now she realized her hands, too, were covered with the same stickiness.

She reached the panel of switches and pushed them all on at once. Light flooded the hall and the curved staircase. Hannah blinked, her eyes smarting with the brightness. She looked down at her hands. They were bright with blood. Blood oozed down the bare steps, and crawled like obscene worms onto the wide planks of the floor. Hannah's eyes followed the gruesome trail to the top of the stairs. "Gott in Himmel!" Hannah choked out the words as she looked at a horrific sight. On the landing lay her friend, Annette Adams. A butcher knife protruded from her still, unmoving chest.

CHAPTER TWO

Caroline Miller drove her Mercury Sable as fast as she could, zipping over the back roads of Lancaster County at breakneck speed, slowing only when she saw an Amish, horse-drawn vehicle on the road.

Her grandmother, Hannah Miller, Granny Hanny to almost everyone in the county, called Caroline as soon as she notified 911.

"Carrie," Hannah said, in a voice so shaky that Caroline didn't recognize it for a minute. "Carrie, something awful has happened... Nettie Adams is dead. I found her...murdered."

"Where are you Granny?" Caroline almost shouted, thinking if Nettie was killed by some intruder, he might still be nearby and her grandmother could be in danger.

Hannah followed Caroline's reasoning. "No one is here now, Carrie. Whoever did this is gone. Nettie's legs were already showing what they call in the detective stories, postmortem lividity. That means she'd been dead for a while, and I found bloody footprints on the back stairs, and leading out to the yard and off into the field.

5

"First Bob, now this. Poor Nettie...maybe she was not perfect, but ..." Hannah broke off.

"Call the police, Gran. Just dial 911."

"I already did."

"Good. Wait outside. Okay? I'll be there as soon as I can. And Gran, don't touch anything."

"I know." Hannah had replied, uncharacteristically meek.

Twenty minutes later Caroline pulled her car in behind two fire trucks and a rescue squad ambulance. Everyone but the police, Caroline thought. "Figures", she muttered aloud, remembering the awkward performance of the local township police when her brother, Josh, was accused of murder the previous spring.

Her grandmother, Hannah, sat on the porch steps, grimly clutching a large white bundle. As Caroline approached her, she saw bloody hand prints on the once pristine package. Hannah's hands were smeared with blood, and small bloody footprints led from the house to where she sat.

"Oh, Granny," Caroline cried, enfolding Hannah, package and all, in her arms.

Hannah let herself be comforted for a moment, and Caroline felt the tension in her grandmother's shoulders relax slightly.

"What happened, Granny?"

Hannah told her in a terse voice,. "It is one thing, Carrie, to see a person die peacefully, or even from an accident. The Lord knows I have seen plenty of dead people already, and read all sorts of mysteries from the library, but this..." she shuddered. "Nettie must have tried hard to get away. Ach, Nettie of all people; she was so afraid of pain. They used to tranquilize her chust to go to the dentist."

Caroline let her grandmother talk, knowing it was the best thing she could do at the moment.

"Nettie must have put up a good fight. Ach, Carrie, there was blood everywhere upstairs. This is chust..." Sirens wailed, interrupting her.

Three police cars and a police van tore up the driveway.

"That's most of the police in the township," Caroline commented.

In rural, heavily Amish, Chelsea township the main job of the police was to deal with accidents. Most involved buggies and cars. While the Amish knew how dangerous cars were to their horse drawn vehicles, the automobile drivers didn't always. All it took was a bit of driver inattention or excessive speed to spook a horse, or come too close to a buggy hugging the shoulder of the road. Every Amish person knew someone who had been injured or killed from unequal battles between automobile and buggy. But violent crime was a rarity.

As the cars pulled to a stop, Chelsea's Acting Police Chief, Kiel Benton emerged from the first one. He was in charge of the 10-man force. Since the recent death of the longtime chief, Ted Rowland from a heart attack, Benton was the senior staff member at age 30.

Since Caroline had last seen him, Benton had less hair and more paunch. Hannah called him the beige man because Benton's hair, eyes and skin were an identical shade of sandy brown.

"Mrs. Miller, sorry you had to be the one to stumble on this." He nodded to Caroline. "Ms. Miller," he acknowledged her presence as briefly as good manners would allow. He obviously hadn't forgotten their first encounter when he was shown up by Caroline, with more than a bit of help from Hannah. Neither had Caroline. She saw little reason to think the intervening months had miraculously turned Benton into a sharp witted detective.

"Mrs. Miller, as soon as I get my men going, I'll need a statement. If you are feeling all right, could you stay?"

His manner towards Hannah was so deferential, Caroline had the urge to smile. Hannah Miller was not only tougher than she looked, but ten times the detective he was. Despite her clandestine habit of reading mystery books from the library, she hadn't learned how to be an investigator strictly from her fictional friends. Most of Hannah's luck with solving mysteries came from a combination of intellect and intuition.

"Of course I am all right, Kiel Benton, and certainly I will stay. Nettie was my friend. I want to find out who killed her chust much as the police do."

"Yes, Ma'am," Benton answered, reddening. Then he looked at Hannah's hands. "Is that your blood on your hands, or the deceased's?"

"Well, it is not mine. Whether it's Nettie's or whoever killed her, or both, I do not know. I am leaving that part to you to find out. I am no pathologist. There is plenty more on the floor where this came from for you to analyze."

Again Benton looked disconcerted. Caroline was almost beginning to feel sorry for him. He kept making the same mistake. Because Granny was Amish, nearly seventy years old and barely five feet tall, he was both underestimating her, and, worse in Gran's book, patronizing her. If there was one thing that stirred Hannah up, it was to be patronized. Caroline thought the man was an awfully slow learner if he hadn't figured that out from his earlier meetings with Hannah.

"No. I mean yes, ma'am," he said, escaping into the house.

Granny and Caroline sat in Caroline's car waiting for Benton.

"I hate to have the police be the ones to tell Kaitlin or Jen about this, seems so... unfeeling," Hannah said, pronouncing the "J" in Jen like a "ch". Normally, Hannah spoke perfectly accented English, formally eschewing even contractions. Only in moments of stress did she lapse into a

Pennsylvania Dutch accent, liberally sprinkled with "Dutch" and German words.

"Well, Gran, it's their job to notify the next of kin, which would be Kaitlin. Considering she's not quite eighteen, they will probably tell Peter, then let him tell Kate. After all, he is her father, and despite the fact he and Nettie were divorced years and years ago, he should be the one to break the news."

"I suppose," Hannah answered. "But I'd like to be the one to tell Jen. Otherwise, she is apt to hear it on the news. It would be an unfeeling thing to find out like that." To Hannah, being unfeeling was tantamount to a near sin. "Maybe she knows it already. In one of my mystery stories, by Josephine Tey, I believe, one twin always knew when the other was in danger. I do not know about dead," Hannah finished with a visible shiver.

Caroline thought Hannah was beginning to return to normal after her gruesome experience. Caroline knew despite Hannah's feisty retort to Chief Benton, she was still in shock from discovering Annette's body. Her face, usually glowing with good health and high spirits, had been drawn and pale. Now some color was returning to her cheeks. Action was the best medicine for her. And she was right; Jen would quickly know about her sister's death, even if no supernatural powers were involved. Jennet worked at the New York headquarters of a major television network.

"Why don't you ask Benton. I can't imagine he would have any objection. After all you're a close family friend."

It had been a good thirty minutes since Benton had asked them to wait. Caroline had little desire to see either Nettie's body or the death scene, but if they were going to get to a phone so Jen could be notified, she had no choice. She didn't want to subject Hannah to revisiting the house, despite her grandmother's resilience and recovering spirits.

"I'm going to roust Benton out of there so we can go find a phone. If he isn't ready, maybe he can catch up with you at home," Caroline said, starting towards the house.

"Go around to the side then. There is blood all over the front hall. It's probably dry by now, but you may disturb evidence, Carrie."

As Caroline approached the open side door, the raw smell of blood and violent human death permeated the air. Gagging slightly, she tried not to inhale as she called out.

"Lieutenant...I mean... Chief Benton." The last time she met Benton, during the investigation of the death of Susannah Schuler's father, Benton was a Lieutenant.

He appeared promptly in the doorway. "I was just getting back to you," he said, pulling off disposable gloves. He looks a little green himself Caroline thought. "Jeeze, what a mess," he muttered.

8

"You knew Mrs. Adams too?" Benton asked.

"All my life, until I left the area, that is."

"How long ago was that?"

"Nine years. I've only seen Nettie Adams a few times since I came back."

"When was that, Ms. Miller?"

Caroline was getting irritated. He was supposed to be getting a statement from Granny, not wasting time with inanely questioning Caroline. "When was what, Chief? When did I come back or when did I see Nettie?"

"Both."

"I returned here briefly in July, then permanently in September. I first saw Nettie in August...to offer my condolences about her husband."

"Condolences? We don't know he's dead, do we? Looks more like he 'took de money and ran Venezuela' as the Belafonte song goes. Not the first time some guy couldn't take it and wanted a new life. He didn't steal anything. It was his money."

His and Nettie's, Caroline thought.

"At least that's what it looked like before Mrs. Adams was murdered," Benton said. "Now all bets are off. If she wasn't killed by an intruder, then number one suspect has to be the missing Mr. Adams. Right, Counselor?"

With a supreme effort Caroline kept herself from groaning. Benton would jump to an obvious answer. He should be so lucky. And maybe Bob Adams would drive in just about now and confess just to make the Chief's life easy.

"Say Adams is alive," Benton continued, not waiting for Caroline to answer. "What we need to find is a motive. Like, maybe there was a big insurance policy on Mrs. Adams. I'll check it out. You got any other ideas, Ms. Miller?"

Caroline didn't feel like helping him out, but she was almost beginning to feel sorry for him. He really was the most slipshod investigator she'd ever met. He wasn't even following through with his questions. If he had, he'd find out Caroline was Nettie's lawyer and had written her latest will only a few weeks ago. Bob Adams was long gone by then, and couldn't possibly know the contents of the will, so it wouldn't have any bearing on a motive. Still, Benton was pathetically inexperienced. Perhaps it wasn't his fault Chelsea was so peaceful, but what did they teach in criminology courses these days? Or maybe Benton had never taken any.

"If there was an insurance policy, how could Bob collect without resurfacing? And if he did, he'd better have a good alibi. Sorry, but I don't see that as a motive."

"Carrie is right," Hannah said, joining them. "Nettie had more motive to kill Bob than the other way round. He not only left her, but took her money

9

along with his. Besides, I do not think any intruder killed Nettie." She had shed her stiff black bonnet and cape, and stood in the doorway dressed in a black dress and apron with a white prayer cap perched on the back of her thick white hair.

"Why? Even if nothing is missing, maybe Mrs. Adams discovered the intruder before he had time to take anything? Did that occur to you, Mrs. Miller?" Benton looked amused.

Oh, oh, Benton. Not smart, thought Caroline. You are patronizing Granny again. She doesn't like that. Caroline also knew Granny wouldn't make such a definitive statement unless she had reason. Caroline hoped Hannah wouldn't answer with something flip, like "Elementary, my dear Benton."

"Couple of reasons. First one: It obviously wasn't a break-in. Nettie spent a basket of money to put in that fancy alarm. She never left it off, unless she was expecting someone momentarily."

"How about you, Granny?" Caroline asked hastily. She wanted to stop Granny before she made herself look silly in front of the Chief. "Wasn't Nettie expecting you?"

Hannah eyed her granddaughter. "She knew I would be there sometime that day, but not exactly when. I know Nettie; there is, er, was no way she would leave that alarm off."

"Okay, that makes sense," Benton conceded. "And?"

"Next, I would say Nettie was expecting someone else besides me. She was dressed up already. Normally she would not even be out of her nightie before noon. She was one to do housework in her robe. I have even seen her sweeping the porch before she got dressed. I was over to her house do not know how many times. She would not have gotten dressed for me. Yet when I found her...body..., she was all dressed up, fancy-like. Nettie Adams knew whoever killed her."

"Impressive reasoning, Mrs. Miller."

"Not really. Chust that I knew her well. Now, I would not think of telling you how to conduct your investigation, Kiel Benton. But if I was doing the investigating, I would forget an intruder. Neither would I be looking for Bob Adams. Nope, I would be looking for a suspect with a motive." Hannah looked thoughtful, then shook her head vigorously up and down, causing the ribbons on her prayer cap to bounce. "Yah, there are chust a few other folks around here with real good reasons to want Nettie Adams dead."

CHAPTER THREE

"Who?" Benton blurted.

"Don't worry, I will tell you. Course what I know is not only facts; lots of it is gossip. You will have to check it all out."

"Yes. Of course, Ma'am."

Why did Hannah feel like she was teaching a class? Maybe she was. If Kiel Benton had read as much as she had on crime solving, he would know the finer points of investigation. Oh, well, guess she would have to help. Again. But not until she called Jen.

"First, would you mind if I was the one to notify Nettie Adams' sister in New York? Think the news would fall easier on her coming from a friend."

"I don't have any objection," Benton replied.

"I suppose you will want to get my statement while the details are fresh in my mind. I am an old woman and my memory might be not as good as it once was." Over his shoulder, Hannah saw Carrie roll her blue eyes.

"Then you'll let me know about the others who had a motive..." Benton said.

Hannah thought Benton's look was akin to Daisy, her kitten when the little cat spied Hannah fixing dinner -anxious and hungry-, bordering on starving already.

"Of course. So, let us get on with this statement. We can sit in the car. It is more restful for me there."

Caroline was heading towards her car, her thick blond hair bouncing on shoulders shaking with mirth. Hannah knew she would get a lecture from her granddaughter later.

Despite being saddened at Nettie's death, Hannah would waste little time grieving. That was not her way. She knew Nettie was in a better place. Grieving would not bring her back. All she could do for her old friend now was to do what she could to bring her killer to justice.

Hannah couldn't resist pulling Benton's chain. She hadn't forgiven him for assuming her grandson, Joshua was a murderer, and refusing to conduct a proper investigation. She remembered only too well Benton's plodding ineptness and bullheadedness. If she and Carrie hadn't involved themselves in the investigation, Joshua would be in jail instead of getting married next month. Still and all, Hannah thought, Benton is sort of pitiful. Left on his own, he might never find Nettie's murderer. He needs all the help he can get. She and Carrie would have to take a hand.

As Hannah turned to follow Caroline to the car, the telephone, just inside the house's open door, began to ring.

Benton made no move to answer it. "There's a machine there. I'll let it pick up. Might be something interesting. Having the police answer might spook someone off."

Maybe he is learning something, Hannah thought.

"Nettie, Nettie, you there?" A shrill voice demanded.

Hannah recognized it as Sadie Shoop, one of two sisters who lived down the road. Hannah called them the Snoop Sisters; not much went on without Annie and Sadie knowing about it. "You all right? What are all the emergency vehicles doing headed down there? Answer, Nettie!" she demanded.

"You know who that is?" Benton asked Hannah.

She nodded. "Sadie Shoop. Lives down 'bout a half mile towards town."

"Call us, Nettie, soon as you get there," Sadie ordered, and then hung up.

"Amish?" Benton asked.

"No, Plain though. Mennonite. She and her sister, Annie both. They are what you "English" call old maids. We say 'en alt maed'"".

"Sounds about the same to me. Are they just neighbors?"

"They do, er, did, some work for Nettie. They restore antique quilts. Real old ones. It is quite an art, you know."

"If you say so, Mrs. Miller. You are the expert there."

Caroline stood by the car, pointedly looking at her watch. "Your granddaughter looks like she wants to get out of here. Can't blame her," Benton said. "Let's get your statement before the coroner gets here. You have any problem with talking into a tape recorder?"

"Not as long as it is battery operated, and it does not belong to me," Hannah answered. "I don't mind observing your "English" gadgets, but using anything powered by electricity coming in on the lines is a bad habit to get into. One thing leads to another. Before you know it, all our kids are watching MTV."

Benton's eyebrows shot up. "Mind if I ask how you know about MTV?"

"Just said it was a bad habit to get into. I did not say I never did it. But only when I am a guest in an "English" home, or happen to see it at a store."

"Interesting. Now about the statement..." Benton turned towards the police cruiser. "I'll grab the recorder and meet you at your granddaughter's car."

A few minutes later, the Chief was interviewing Hannah.

"What did you do after you saw the body, Mrs. Miller?"

"Made sure she was dead. Though I did not have much doubt. There was blood everywhere, and a mighty big knife in Nettie's chest. She did not look like she was breathing. I got closer, I saw her eyes open, staring. To be sure, I checked the carotid pulse. Nothing. Other than that, I didn't touch anything."

"You heard nothing? No doors slamming, no car?"

"Nothing."

"Did you observe anything else? About the body? The house?"

"Well, postmortem lividity was beginning in Nettie's feet. Figured it had to have been at least 20 minutes, but not much longer."

"Why not much longer?" Benton asked.

"Two things. Nettie was still warm...she had color in her lips and face. Then there was the spilled blood. It was just starting to clot. I would say she was killed somewhere between 20-30 minutes before I arrived."

Benton looked as impressed as Hannah supposed he would be.

"You read a lot of books, right, Mrs. Miller?"

"Yes, I do. A person can learn a lot that way, Kiel Benton." Although she didn't say so, Hannah hoped he would profit by her example. A little more knowledge would be helpful in his line of work.

"Hmm," Benton looked thoughtful. "What else did you observe?

"I would say the killer got Nettie off guard, then pulled a knife on her. She ran, but did not fight. There was no blood under her nails. I looked."

"I see," Benton said. "Very thorough, Mrs. Miller. Incidentally before you tell me to, I've told my men to make casts of the footprints and tire tracks."

"I am sure you know your business, Chief Kiel Benton. I am just here to help; if you need me," Hannah answered, using his title even though the Amish avoided titles, feeling them to be unnecessary.

"Thank you for the offer, Mrs. Miller. I never turn down help. I promised you could make your calls, so go ahead. Mind if I drop by after I'm through here? I want to know who may have had something against the deceased."

"I will be stopping at my granddaughter's to make my calls. Then you will find me at my house, the little one attached to the big one."

"I remember, Mrs. Miller. See you later," he said.

Fifteen minutes later, Hannah and Caroline were in the living room of Caroline's condominium. Hannah admired the way Caroline decorated it; she had used lots of bright, floral prints with a mix furniture which she had painted white. Sunlight streamed into the living room.

"I do not relish telling Jen, Carrie, but best it come from me rather than from a stranger over the airwaves, or whatever they are called," Hannah said, eyeing the telephone on the table alongside her chair.

"I'll get her on the phone, Gran. I have her private number. I made a note of it when we had lunch while I was living in New York," Caroline said, picking up the phone and rapidly punching in the numbers. "Let's hope she's there." Caroline handed the phone back to Hannah.

Jennet Hope wasn't in her office, and by the time she was located and returned Hannah's call, four hours had passed.

"Hannah, hello," Jennet Hope's melodious voice said. "Sorry it took me so long to get back to you. I was filming a show. How are you? Nothing's wrong there, is it?"

"I am afraid so, Jen. I have something sad to tell you. Nettie is dead," Hannah announced, dispensing in the Amish way with the useless "How are you?" She didn't see much point in trying to soften the news; there was no way to do that anyhow. She was sure Jen would take it hard no matter what. Best get it over with.

Hannah heard a gasp at the other end of the line. "Oh, Granny, no! How...?" She broke off with a small sob.

"Somebody came into the house and killed her, Jen. I am so sorry, dear." Jennet recovered her voice. "Who?"

"The police are trying to find that out now. They have no suspects yet."

"I'll get there as soon as I can, Granny. But, I don't want to stay at Nettie's."

"No, of course not, Jen. You can stay with Carrie. She would be glad to have you." Hannah looked at Caroline who shook her head in assent. "You could come to my place, but living without electricity might be a burden for you," Hannah said, thinking of hair dryers, curling irons and all the other paraphernalia "English" women traveled with.

"Thank you, Granny. Oh, God... Kaitlin. Has anyone told her yet?"

"Peter is going to. Let me put Carrie on, Jen; she can give you directions to her house," Hannah said, passing the phone to Caroline.

After expressing her sympathy, Caroline told Jennet where she lived, then handed the phone back to Hannah.

"About the arrangements. What happens now when it's ...murder?" Jen asked with a catch in her voice.

"The coroner will decide when the body can be released," Hannah answered gently. "We will know more tomorrow. Don't worry. We will be here to help you."

"Thank you for everything, Granny. I'll be there sometime this evening," Jennet said, hanging up the phone.

"I am not sure why, Carrie, but I was expecting hysterics from Jen. She sounded upset, but in control."

"She's probably in shock, or denial, as they say these days."

"I suppose," Hannah said thoughtfully. "It is unlikely Jen could be involved in Nettie's murder. After all, she would barely have had time to get back to New York by now, let alone be filming a show. Right?" Hannah looked at her granddaughter quizzically.

"Good question, Granny. I was wondering that myself. I assume you want me to find out?"

"You bet I do. I sure do hate thinking Jen might be involved..."

"I know, but everyone is a suspect until proven otherwise. Including Jen."

"Including Jen," Hannah said, shaking her head sadly.

15

CHAPTER FOUR

Caroline telephoned Benton to have him meet Hannah at five o'clock at Caroline's condominium.

She and Hannah had also made several other calls. One was to Caroline's father, Daniel, at his dairy to break the news about Nettie and tell him Hannah would be with Caroline. Of the others to neighbors and friends, the most distressing call was to Peter Drew, Nettie's ex-husband and the father of Nettie's only child, seventeen year-old Kaitlin.

The police had already called him. "Peter took this harder than I would have expected," Hannah commented. "Course hearing poor Nettie was murdered is enough to shock anybody. Guess, too, he was thinking of Kaitlin's reaction. First he has to find her. Said he had no idea where she was, but she was supposed to be back tonight."

"It won't be easy telling her."

"I know. Despite everything, Nettie was her mother."

"What happened between Nettie and Kate, Granny?"

"I am not really sure, but it seemed to start when Nettie married Bob Adams. Maybe a new husband and a teenage daughter were too much for Nettie. You know how high-strung she was."

"Nettie had quite a temper. I remember seeing her lose it a couple of times. I was embarrassed both for her and the unlucky person she was mad at."

"We all have our faults," Hannah said. "Nettie's temper was hers. She was always kind to me."

"That wouldn't be too hard."

"There are some who would not say that," Hannah smiled.

"I think you ought to lie down until Benton gets here," Caroline said as she cleared off the table from their late lunch. She didn't like the dark shadows that had settled under Hannah's eyes. Her grandmother looked tired.

"Don't be silly, Carrie. When did you last see me nap?"

"Formally? Never, but I have seen you sneak naps plenty of times."

"Cat naps, just resting my eyes. I never nap. Seriously, Carrie, I'm too fergelschterd to nap," Hannah said, using the Pennsylvania Dutch word for upset. Slipping into Pennsylvania Dutch was something she rarely did, believing it was rude to speak "Dutch" in front of an Englisher. Despite the fact Caroline was her granddaughter and was raised Amish, she was considered English now.

"I understand," Caroline said. "I'm keyed up,too, but who knows how late we'll be up waiting for Jen? I wish you'd let me take you home after Benton gets through."

"Nope. Would not be fitting if I was not here when Jennet arrives. Other than Kate, she has no relatives. I will have to fill in as a family for her."

"I'm surprised Jen never married. I don't suppose her career left her any time. Or she didn't want it to."

"Marrying is not easy, or so you tell me every time I ask about Stephen or that Bryce Jordan fellow you work for."

Hannah had a well deserved reputation among the Amish as a matchmaker. Her purpose wasn't simply to marry people off indiscriminately. When her two middle sons, Christopher and Leif (Since there were no restrictions against naming children any name the parents liked, and except for her eldest, Daniel- named after his grandfather- Hannah named her children and her pets after whatever she was reading at the time. The boys' names were a result of her discovering explorers), moved to an Amish settlement in Kentucky where farmland was more affordable than in Lancaster County, Hannah was surprisingly accepting of their decisions.

She knew the incidence of genetic defects among Amish babies was reaching an alarming rate. "Too much intermarrying among kin, just like I have been trying to tell 'em for years," she announced to everyone who would listen.

It wasn't long before Hannah arranged for her youngest unmarried daughters, Victoria and Regina (named after Hannah's foray into the literary world of British royalty) to work as mother's helpers when her sons' wives had their latest babies. Hannah gave each daughter a month before she arrived for a visit, ostensibly to see the baby, but in reality to look over the eligible young men.

Not that her daughters needed much help; Vickie and Gina were blond and lively, petite replicas of their mother. Both were married to Amish Kentuckians by November of those years.

Other Amish families followed Hannah's lead, and marriages between settlements in Indiana, Ohio, Pennsylvania and Kentucky were now commonplace and letters flew back and forth like birds on the wing. In addition to using mail to communicate, Amish families relied heavily on the "Budget," a weekly newspaper which listed day-to-day activities and vital statistics for Amish and Mennonite families from South America to Canada.

Still, like many happily married people, (Hannah's own satisfying marriage of forty years ended when her husband Levi died), she believed that being married is better than being single. Seeing anyone single left her with an overwhelming desire to "fix 'em up".

"Don't even think about it, Granny. Raising an almost eight- year-old, keeping up with my law practice, and getting involved with your shenanigans is all I can handle right now. Watch out, or I'll start fixing you up with some old Amish widower."

"Just what I need. I would drive the poor man to an early grave. No man I know would put up with me. And I, sure as can be, would not be a dutiful wife. No, I…"

The doorbell rang, interrupting Hannah.

"Probably Chief Benton. He's early," Caroline said, going to answer the bell.

Instead of the chief, she opened the door to Annie and Sadie Shoop.

"Where is Hannah?" Sadie, the eldest demanded, her head craning around Caroline to look inside the room.

"What's happened to Nettie?" Annie Shoop asked. "I know it's something terrible. Nobody will tell me anything. The police won't. Daniel tells me Hannah's here with you." Annie's words poured out in a wail.

"I'm here, girls," Hannah said. "Was just about to call you. Needed to get to the relatives first. Come in," she said unnecessarily. The sisters were already in the room and looming over the tiny Amishwoman.

18

At ages 45 and 42, neither sister had ever married. Members of a moderately conservative Mennonite sect, they lived in a dilapidated, 150 year-old farmhouse their parents built. It bordered one side of the Adams' property. Hannah had known them, like almost everyone else in Chelsea township younger than she was, all their lives.

When Caroline was a child, she thought the Shoop sisters looked like two animals; Sadie was a giant dog, and Annie a scrawny cat. She still did.

With her lugubrious eyes, down turned mouth, large ears and bushy eyebrows, Sadie resembled something between an Airedale and a basset hound. Sadie, the eldest was four inches taller and thirty pounds heavier than Annie.

Annie was timid, and although of average height, delicate looking, with a small pointed chin and large, almond shaped eyes. Despite looking as if she was expecting to be kicked at any moment, she was a pretty woman with high cheekbones and a soft mouth.

The sisters were dressed much alike in pastel printed dresses with modest, high necklines and mid-length hemlines. Their naturally wavy dark blond hair was wound into buns and covered by small, Mennonite prayer caps. Caroline thought they acted as though life was something to be endured on their way to Heaven.

The sisters' favorite activity was finding out what other people were doing. Even Hannah, who tried hard to be charitable, often found her patience sorely tried by Annie and Sadie.

The best she could say in their behalf is that they were wonderful craftswomen. The sisters were experts in restoration, mending antique quilts with minute stitches and painstaking attention to original detail. Nettie, whose antique shop specialized in antique quilts, employed the Shoops full-time.

"It is bad news. Nettie is dead," Hannah said to the sisters who sat perched on the edge of Caroline's flowered sofa.

"Oh, no!" Annie shrieked, sounding like Daisy when her tail was stepped on..

Hannah gave Annie a minute to compose herself. The shrieking turned into wailing, then into blubbering sobs. "All right, Annie, get a hold on yourself." Instantly Annie quieted down, sniffling into a handkerchief. Sadie simply sat stone-still. Not a flicker of emotion crossed her face, nor did she attempt to comfort her sister. The only visible reaction was that the color drained from her normally ruddy complexion.

Hannah succinctly told them about finding Nettie and notifying the authorities. Caroline noticed Hannah didn't share her theory that Nettie knew her killer. Nor did she divulge to the sisters anything more than the basic facts. Hannah was aware of the sisters' penchant for gossip.

"This is the worst thing that's ever happened to us," Annie said in a dramatic voice. "Worse than Bob, already. First B-B-Bob, now her. What if I had been the one to find the body? I could have easily, living right next door and all."

"Hush up, Annie. Stop carrying on so," Sadie told her sister. Sadie then launched into a barrage of questions directed at Hannah. "Are there any suspects? Did he leave any clues?"

Hannah answered as briefly and quickly as she could. "I cannot say what the police found or think. They do not confide in me."

"When's Jennet coming? What about the funeral?"

"Tonight, late. What she does about the funeral is up to her. I will let you know about the funeral soon as it is arranged."

Hannah was answering more and more brusquely. Talk about suffering fools, Caroline thought. Granny's doing a lot better than I would. I'd have those two out on their rears by now.

"What dress do you think Nettie would like to be buried in?" Annie, asked leaning forward.

"Annie, I have no idea what dress Nettie would like to be buried in." Hannah looked at Caroline with a pained expression. Looking at the clock, Caroline noticed it was almost five o'clock. Benton would be arriving anytime. Time to help Hannah get rid of the sisters.

Caroline got up and began to noisily load the dishwasher.

"Looks like Carrie needs my help. I will have Carrie phone you soon as I know anything about the funeral." Hannah walked to the door and opened it. Even the sisters couldn't ignore the dismissal.

After they left, Hannah asked to take over loading the dishwasher, a task she enjoyed doing. Hannah was fascinated by modern gadgets, especially those in Caroline's new kitchen. Whether it was running the garbage disposal, or cooking in the microwave, Hannah was loathe to let anyone else take over in the kitchen when she was around.

"Thought they would never go," Hannah said with an audible sigh of relief. "This may not sound too kind, Carrie, but those two could drive a body crazy. Annie was wailing, not so much about poor Nettie, but saying it was just lucky she didn't find the body. And saying that was the worse thing every happened to her. And how how about the worst thing ever to happen to Nettie. Can you believe it?"

"Easily, Gran. I've known Annie all my life; she overreacts when she's disturbed."

"Does not draw a difference between a mouse in her house and a murder. She gets this way over anything and everything. I've always thought the woman was a bit off plumb," Hannah said, shaking her head so vigorously the ties on her white prayer cap danced and bobbed like whitecaps.

"And Sadie?" Caroline asked. "What did you think of her reaction?"

"Like you would expect. Her reaction was no reaction. Yet, had to know every detail. Course I am sure you noticed I did not share too much. I do not think Kiel Benton would appreciate the 'Snoop Sisters' spreading rumors all over. Specially when they would be distorted in no time flat."

"I doubt you or anyone else can stop them."

"Nope, do not suppose so. Leastwise I will not help them. Problem with those two is they need to get a life."

"Granny, where do you pick up your slang? I swear you know more colloquialisms than I do."

"I would think so, Carrie. I am an awful eavesdropper, you know. And probably a bigger snoop than the sisters. I, however, know how to keep my mouth shut."

"That's what makes you a good detective."

"All the mystery reading I do does not hurt. Just call me Hannah Miller, Amish bloodhound," she giggled.

"Granny, I think we are getting slap-happy."

"Getting? Better said: gotten." Hannah laughed, flopping into a large terra cotta-colored chair. Her feet dangled over the edge like a child's.

Caroline thought her grandmother looked like a flower in a pot, but refrained from saying so. Hannah was sensitive about her small stature.

With a deep sigh, Hannah was instantly asleep.

Caroline wondered how Hannah could take even a cat nap given the experience she had been through. *I don't think it's really hit her, and she's going to have to relive it when Benton gets here. Thank God she is asleep; she's going to need all the rest she can get to go through the horror of discovering Nettie's body all over again.* Caroline shivered involuntarily.

Hannah hadn't been asleep more than five minutes when the doorbell rang again.

This time it was Chief Benton at the door, accompanied by a policewoman with a tape recorder.

CHAPTER FIVE

Benton introduced the policewoman, Sergeant Peg McCoy. She doubled as a stenographer and was going to take Hannah's statement. "Thought you were going home, Mrs. Miller," he commented.

Hannah thought Benton would be well served by sticking to business, but just smiled placidly. "Have to be here to wait for Jennet Hope."

"Ah, yes, Mrs. Adams' sister. Everybody around here knows about Jennet Hope."

"You watch her show?" Hannah asked.

"I have, just out of curiosity. When is she supposed to get here, Mrs. Miller? I'll need to talk to her."

"She is driving in sometime later tonight," Hannah answered.

"Staying with you?"

"No, with Carrie, here."

Benton turned to Caroline. "Have her call the station tomorrow. Okay?"

"I will."

Benton had Hannah repeat what she'd told him earlier. "Okay, Mrs. Miller, who are the people who might have had a reason to see Mrs. Adams dead?"

"Nettie was an old friend, but in truth she was not well-liked by a lot of folks, Chief. Real short tempered and irritable. I used to tell her, but she did not listen to me. Maybe she could not help it."

Hannah felt she should somehow defend Nettie, or at least explain her faults. The image of Nettie as a child kept getting in Hannah's way. Adorable, with bouncing curls and innocent blue eyes, Nettie was the antithesis of the angel she resembled. She was the trouble maker, leading not only her twin, Jennet, into trouble, but Hannah's kids as well.

The twins' father, Tom Hope was a wonderful doctor but a failure as a father. The man had no idea how to care for one child, let alone two. He gave up and let them have anything they wanted. Jennet only wanted to please; Nettie wanted everything else, especially anything someone else had. The Hopes went through housekeeper after housekeeper. Nettie wore them down, then broke them like used crayons pressed too hard on paper.

Hannah saw behind the naughty girl to the needy, motherless child. In spite of Nettie's deblishness, Hannah couldn't turn her away. Instead she made room for the twins in her generous heart. Both girls spent most of their summers at Hannah's house.

There was just so much Hannah's love and concern could help. Nettie had an irrational, untamed streak that defied anything Hannah did for her. Nettie's personality traits followed her into adulthood. Hannah tried to see the sunshine and ignore the shadows, but with Nettie it was often nearly impossible.

"I see," Benton answered. But who specifically would hate Annette Adams enough to kill her? Name names please."

"Just about anybody who dealt in a business way with her held some grudge. She used to tell me about them. Since I knew you would want names, I wrote them down, sort of in order of who I thought the most likely suspects were. I included motives." She handed him a piece of neatly ruled paper with a dozen entries.

Benton studied it for a minute, then looked up. "I'll read them aloud for Peg," he said, glancing at the policewoman. "Then I'll ask you about each. Okay?"

Hannah nodded.

Benton started down the list she had prepared.

"Dr. Peter Drew, her ex-husband? Isn't he a dentist over in Gordonsville?"

"That's the one. Peter and Nettie had a pretty bitter divorce. Later, he sued Nettie for custody of their daughter. Won, too. Nettie detested him, and according to her, the feeling was mutual.

"Ever hear him say anything threatening?"

"Yes, one day at Nettie's antique store. It was right before the custody trial. Nettie and Peter were in the back room when all of a sudden it started. Never have I heard such screaming and yelling; it was something fierce." Hannah shook her head, as if she was attempting to wipe out the noise. "I was the only one in the shop at the time. Peter said someday she'd get what was coming to her; if it took forever, he'd see to it."

"When was that?"

"Four years ago."

"But you said he sued her?"

"Yes, but Nettie fought back; she threatened to bring up his past. Peter was a recovering alcoholic; spent some time in the county jail for drunk driving. Nobody knew about it. It happened years and years ago, but he was afraid it would be held against him by folks. Folks are afraid enough of going to the dentist, even a sober one. He begged Nettie not to ruin him."

"And?"

"And she just laughed at him, said 'all's fair in love and war.' Awful expression. That is when the yelling started. Anyhow, she did bring his past up in court. The judge gave the daughter, Kaitlin, nicknamed Kate, to him just the same."

"Do you know why the judge decided in his favor?"

"Kaitlin got on the stand and said she did not want anything to do with her mother. She said she hated Nettie."

"Whew. That's rough. How old was the daughter then?"

"Thirteen."

"How does she feel about her mother now?"

"You will have to ask her. All I know is Nettie had not seen her in four years. Now it is too late for a reconciliation," Hannah said. She shook her head.

"I see why you also named Kaitlin Drew on your list of suspects."

"She is not even eighteen, but…"

"Murderers are getting younger and younger. What do you know about the girl now?"

"Only that her father has had one hard time managing her. She dropped out of high school. Works in a record store at Park City Mall in Lancaster," Hannah answered, watching Peg Mc Coy's fingers fly across her steno pad. "Do you know the name of the place, Carrie?"

"It's The Disc Den," Caroline answered.

"I'll check her out, but unless the girl is an Amazon, she didn't kill her mother. The bloody footprints were made by a size 12 shoe. Besides your footprints, size 4 ½, there were only one set of footprints, those size 12 prints," Benton said, sitting back in his chair. "That eliminates about three quarters of your suspect list, Mrs. Miller."

"Excepting if a person had an accomplice maybe..." Hannah paused, her eyebrows raising quizzically. "Maybe there could be two persons involved, the one who actually stabbed Nettie, and another who left before there was any blood to make footprints." Hannah didn't mention the possibility of a hired killer, but she had thought of it.

"I guess," Benton said, reddening slightly.

"Then we could get on with the other names on my list?"

"Right," Benton said, reddening more.

Hannah didn't want to keep showing Kiel Benton up, but the fellow was hopeless, just hopeless. She was only trying to help him out. Lord knows he needed help, all he could get.

"Despite what you said at the murder scene, I see Bob Adams' name on this list," Benton said.

"I still do not think it was him. No motive I can see, but... he did walk out on Nettie. There may have been something between the Adams I was not told."

"Tell me what you do know about the relationship between the deceased and the missing husband, Bob Adams."

"Bob Adams was a house builder, a contractor as the English say. I imagine you know this, Chief, having investigated his disappearance?"

"Yes, but go ahead, Mrs. Miller."

"He and Nettie met when he built an addition to her antique shop, Flying Needles. Bob was a bit younger than Nettie. To be exact, he was fifteen years younger.

"As far as anyone knew, they were happy...built the new house and all. I knew Nettie 'bout as well as anyone round here and I never knew anything different. Guess they were married about five years when he just drove off last summer."

Benton looked thoughtful. "Never to be seen again. And why? We sure as heck couldn't find a trace of him, nor any reason he should want to drop from sight."

"Maybe he found some young girl. You know cherchez la femme. Bob liked women, maybe a little too much," Hannah said, shrugging her shoulders.

Both Benton and the policewoman looked at Hannah with almost identical quizzical looks.

"Oh, do not look so surprised, you two. I may be an Amish granny, but I know what goes on in the English world. I sure cannot think of any other reason why he would clean out the bank account and up and leave. His business was going fine. There were no debts. It is a puzzle."

"When it looks like a guy in his right mind wants to get lost and the police have no indication of a crime being committed, we can't do much to find a missing person."

"I understand. So did Nettie. That fancy private investigator she hired did not come up with a thing either."

"I didn't know she hired one," Benton said. "Do you remember his name?"

"Don't think Nettie said. Seems to me she mentioned he came from down Philadelphia way. That's all I recall."

"No problem; if he didn't come up with anything, his name doesn't matter anyway." Benton stretched, stifling a yawn.

"I suppose you could find out his name easy enough. Nettie probably wrote him a check," Hannah said.

"Yeah, she probably would have," Benton said, stifling a yawn.

The rest of the names on Hannah's list were various tradesmen and locals who had once had minor feuds with Nettie. Benton appeared to discount them.

"The woman who phoned while we were at the scene, the neighbor, Sadie Shoop? You said she and her sister worked for the deceased."

"Yes."

"Did she get along with the deceased?"

Hannah wished Benton would stop calling Nettie the deceased. "After a fashion - like strange bedfellows."

"How's that?" Benton looked puzzled, like he'd never heard the expression. Carrie was always telling Hannah she shouldn't use clichés and aphorisms. Too much reading had imprinted them on Hannah's syntax.

"The girls, the Shoop sisters, worked for Nettie; Nettie never made any secret of the fact she did not care for them much. It was a business matter; Nettie needed their skills, the girls needed the work. They thought their services were worth more money and were always grumbling they thought Nettie worked them like slaves. I do not know too many who would have put up with them. Far as I know Nettie paid them fair wages," Hannah said, sneaking a furtive look at the large man's pocket watch she had pinned to her pocket. She would just as soon Benton be long gone before Jennet arrived. Tomorrow was soon enough for her to be questioned. "It was Nettie who gave them the nickname of the Snoop Sisters. Annie and Sadie are what the English call busy bodies."

"The Amish don't have busy bodies?"

"You bet," Hannah laughed. "We just do not call them that; that's the only difference."

"You say the deceased and the Shoop women didn't have much use for each other, but that was it?"

"Annie and Sadie did not make my list, Chief."

"Okay, but I have to check names, on and off your list."

"Of course, Chief, any good detective would. I hardly know everything."

"If you did, I could ask you the murderer's name, Mrs. Miller." Benton was smiling like he was indulging a precocious child. Hannah said a quick prayer for patience.

"And if I knew, I would tell you, Kiel Benton. It would save us all a lot of work," she said, her prayer gone unanswered.

CHAPTER SIX

Caroline stared at her grandmother intently in the hopes Hannah would read her mind. *Back off, Granny. Give the guy a chance. You are not always going to be able to solve his cases for him. Let him make his own mistakes.*

As an attorney who had only been practicing a few years herself, Caroline remembered what it was like to be in a bit over her head. She learned as much in that kind of panic situation as she did when a more experienced lawyer helped her.

The phone temporarily stopped Benton. Caroline answered.

"It's for you, Chief," she said, handing him the cordless phone.

"What? When was that? No, I better go out there and talk to them myself. Tell Miles I'll be there in twenty minutes. And, Lu, send somebody out here to pick up McCoy. We're through here, and she's off duty." He handed the phone back to Caroline.

"An interesting development. Your Shoop girls just called 911. They reported seeing a prowler around their farm. Could be Mrs. Adams was killed by a stranger after all."

"Are they all right?" Caroline noticed Hannah was concerned enough about Annie and Sadie to ignore his barb.

"I have a couple of men out there; they didn't find anyone. They said Annie Shoop was pretty scared, but her sister was calmer. I'm on my way out there now."

"Mind taking Carrie with you, Chief? I'd go myself, but I need to wait for Jen Hope."

Benton looked surprised at the request. He doesn't know how nervy Granny is, Caroline thought. To paraphrase one of Granny's favorite expressions, Hannah Miller treads where angels fear to go. Granny was also fond of saying: "Ask anyway. All you can get is a no; you're no worse off than if you had not asked."

"The Shoop ladies are probably pretty frightened. Carrie is a friend; she might be a help."

Caroline was standing behind Benton, making faces and shaking her head from side to side. Too late.

Benton shrugged his shoulders. "I suppose it wouldn't hurt anything; might help, actually. I admit I'm not so good with hysterical old maids."

Caroline narrowed her eyes. She was on the verge of saying she wouldn't go, until he said "old maid". Chauvinist! Even though she was barely thirty and once divorced, she got her back up at the term "old maid," when it was used by a man, any man. She wasn't sure if she was more irritated at Benton or at Granny for setting her up.

Granny was getting a little too high handed. Asking for her help was one thing, ordering her around was another. After tonight, this detective stuff Granny was getting her into was going to stop. Caroline had a child, a job, and a reputation to think of. She couldn't go sniffing around the countryside like Granny's bloodhound. Lucky for Hannah, Molly was spending the night with Caroline's ex-husband, Stephen, or Caroline wouldn't be helping out at all. On the other hand, Caroline had to admit she was getting intrigued with the case. It sure beat the wills she'd been writing and estates she'd been settling since going to work for Bryce Jordan's firm. She would help her grandmother this one last time, then no more.

Did Nettie know her killer as Hannah suspected? Or was it a prowler, a stranger? Why would Nettie be dressed up as if she was expecting someone when she was killed? If she had been expecting a visitor, who was it? And surely it couldn't be a coincidence that the Shoops sisters had seen a prowler. Or had they? Maybe their nerves were so frazzled they just thought they'd seen someone.

A brilliant orange sun was sinking on the horizon like an enormous beach ball as Benton unlocked the door of his police car for Caroline. The night was windless, and an icy bite was already in the air, promising frost.

After Caroline and Benton were well on their way to the Shoop farm, he broke the silence.

"Your grandmother is really into this amateur detective stuff, isn't she?"

"She has known Annette Adams since Nettie was a child. I'd say she has a good reason for wanting to see her killer found, Chief."

"Why don't you call me Ben? Everybody else does. I'm not officially chief yet. Depending on what the Township does, I might get lucky and be hired as permanent chief."

"I imagine solving this case would help. Right?"

"You might say that," Benton said. "I'm not complaining about your grandmother's interest, Carrie. Okay if I call you Carrie?"

"I'd prefer Caroline." She decided to try to forget her past grievances with Benton.

"Okay, Caroline. As I was saying, as long as your grandmother doesn't get in the way of an official investigation, I appreciate any help I can get." It sounded like Benton was interested in a fresh start as well. "She seems to hold your brother's troubles last summer against me. Don't understand why; everything turned out okay."

"Umm," Caroline said. She was saved from any further response by their arrival at the Shoop farm.

Located close to the main road at the end of a lane edged with tall fir trees, three quarters of the Shoop house was hidden behind more dense evergreens. For some reason the sisters' father, who built the house, wanted to live in a pine forest. The white painted portion of the farmhouse glowed eerily in the reflected light from a vermillion sky.

A police car with two officers inside was parked in front of the house. Benton walked over to talk to them while Caroline knocked on the door.

The sisters wouldn't open the door, even for Caroline, until they peered out through muslin curtains and saw her.

Once in the house, she was almost knocked down by Annie who threw herself on Caroline, clinging to her. Annie smelled faintly of chlorine-based cleaner.

"Oh, Carrie, there was a huge man prowling around the house! We couldn't see his face, just his back, but he was big. Over six feet, at least." Annie's prayer cap rode rakishly on the side of her head like a small sailboat slipping from its moorings.

"Why don't you sit down, Annie. The police say there's no one here now," Caroline said, leading Annie from the cramped entry hall to the living room and easing her onto a sagging sofa. She sat down beside her.

Every light in the room was on, The room, small and somewhat threadbare, was nonetheless immaculately clean. Like most Pennsylvania Dutch, the sisters were meticulous housekeepers. In fact, with the exception of the electricity and the dozens and dozens of framed photographs on every table and shelf, the home looked much like an Amish home, simple and utilitarian.

"He could come back," Annie moaned, plumping up a handmade quilted pillow and pushing it behind her back.

"That's right; he could come back," Sadie parroted, although in a much calmer voice than her sister. Despite her apparent composure, Sadie was pale, her skin the sallow hue of her ecru cotton dress. Instead of sitting, she paced in front of Caroline and Annie. Finally, she stopped in front of a bookcase filled with photographs and began to rearrange the framed pictures.

"Did you see him, too, Sadie?"

"You bet I did," Sadie answered, her voice growing in volume, like an actress who'd been given her big speech. "He was sneaking across the back, near the pine trees. I didn't get a real good look, but it wasn't anybody who belonged around here. This man was real big, dressed like an English street person, one of those homeless people you see in the cities."

"How so?" Caroline asked.

"You know, dribs and dabs of clothes with none matching. He had blue jeans on, a brown jacket and one of those baseball caps with some kind of advertising writing all over it. He was moving fast, almost running, so I couldn't see what it said."

"Was he old? Young? How about hair color?"

"He looked to be about thirty, maybe. I couldn't see his hair. Like I said, he was wearing a cap."

"With all the police around, whoever you saw is probably miles away by now," Caroline said.

Benton knocked at the door, calling out at the same time.

Both Annie and Sadie jumped. Neither sister made a move to open the door. "I'll get it," Caroline said, opening the door.

"Ladies," he said, acknowledging the sisters who sat on the edge of the faded blue sofa. They looked ready to spring up and dash out the door at the slightest provocation. "My men say there's no sign of anyone on the premises now. Try to relax. You're safe."

"Relax?" Annie said, shrilly. "Nettie's dead, a murderer loose. He may even be here. You don't know. Or he could come back. You don't know."

Sadie glared at Benton. "She's right. Don't tell us we're safe."

"We've made a complete search of the property and have men guarding the house. There's no sign of anyone. I'll leave a patrol here. You really are perfectly safe. Wouldn't you agree, Caroline?"

Well, I asked for this, she thought. Now Benton has put me on the spot. "The Chief is right; you will be well guarded."

31

"If you say so, Carrie," Annie said, quickly looking relieved. "I guess being a lawyer and all, I can trust what you say." .

"If you don't find him, tomorrow I'm going out and get a big dog to guard us," Sadie said.

"Forget a dog," Annie said. I hate dogs. I'm going to get me a gun."

Caroline didn't know whether to laugh or cringe at the thought of Annie Shoop with a gun. She would be more dangerous to herself than to a prowler. Caroline looked at the photographs on the table beside her. They were lined up in their frames like soldiers in formation. There were several of Nettie and Bob Adams, and some of Bob alone. Several must have predated their marriage. Bob looked like a teenager in a few of them. In fact, as Caroline studied them more closely, it looked like some of them were Bob as a small boy. Of course, Hannah had told her Annie used to be Bob's baby sitter or something.

"I don't imagine that will be necessary, ladies," Benton said in a soothing voice. "The prowler is probably in the next state by now." "He won't be back. But we'll keep an eye on you tonight."

Caroline and Benton were out of sight of the Shoop farm before either said anything.

"Do you think they saw someone there, Ben?"

"Absolutely, Caroline. I didn't want to set the ladies off, but my men found footprints. We have to compare the casts, but they sure as heck looked like the same big ones we found at Nettie Adams' house."

"What? And I assured Annie and Sadie they were perfectly safe," Caroline said.

"No, you didn't. You only agreed with me that they would be well guarded. They will be. The Shoop ladies will be fine. The footprints went towards the main road and disappeared. The traffic erased them from the road surface. Our big foot is probably miles away by now."

"Which direction did the footprints come from, Ben? From Nettie's?"

"It was hard to tell. There's so much road surface around. Looks like he walked on the road until he got to the Shoops' farm. Around the house, the ground is soft, but there are a hell of a lot of pine needles. Makes it hard to get a print. We'll go over the place when the light is better. All I can tell is he circled the house a couple of times, then headed away to the road."

"Which road?"

Benton knew Caroline's family lived east of the Shoops and Nettie. "The footprints went west, towards Lancaster. There isn't another farm for fifteen miles."

"That makes me feel a little better. I don't like the idea that the killer may have seen Granny, may know she found the body. Even if he doesn't know one Amish woman from another, the papers are bound to print her name. Everybody around here knows Hannah Miller. It wouldn't be hard to find her."

"You're assuming too much, Caroline. This guy doesn't have wheels. It's not likely he'd chance roaming around Amish farms on foot looking for your grandmother, even if he does think she saw him."

"I guess I'm subscribing to Granny's theory that the things you worry about won't happen. Just the same..."

"If it will make you feel any better, I'll run an extra patrol by your folks' farm until we get this guy. I don't think he'll be out there long. I'd be willing to bet we'll have him by tomorrow."

CHAPTER SEVEN

Hannah heard someone knocking at the door and shook herself awake. She'd been dozing in front the television in Carrie's living room.. Next to a hard day's work, television was the best sleeping pill ever invented.

It couldn't be Jen yet, she thought, looking at the wall clock. She cautiously approached the door and stood on tip-toe to look out the peep hole. Caroline's ex-husband stood on the other side.

Hannah opened the door. "Stephen Brown, what are you doing here? Out to scare an old lady?"

"Never, Granny Hanny," Stephen answered with a smile. "You look a little tired. Did I wake you? You okay?" he asked, scrutinizing her. Although Stephen no longer practiced law, he still had an attorney's way of layering questions one on top of the other.

Hannah's opinion of Stephen had improved vastly since Caroline and her daughter Molly had moved back to Lancaster County. He had turned out to be a wonderful father. In Hannah's estimation, it was enough to qualify him as a mighty fine fellow and nullify his other faults. She was working hard to convince Caroline to share her opinion. So far it was slow going. Very slow going.

"Where's Molly?"

"Home with Maggie," he said, referring to his housekeeper. "I stopped by to pick up her robe. It's turning sort of cold and she forgot it."

"Likely story. You stopped by to see Carrie. She will see right through that one, Stephen Brown. You will have to do better."

"Really, Granny, Molly did forget her robe. Where is Caroline?"

"You haven't heard about Annette Adams?"

Stephen's blank expression was her answer. Hannah told him what had happened.

"Oh, My god! It must have been awful for you to find her body."

"The worst part was that I was not there earlier. I might have saved her."

"Or gotten in the middle of it yourself. Have the police any leads?"

Hannah told him about the intruder the Shoops had reported, and Caroline's trip out to the Shoop farm with Benton.

"You volunteered Carrie? That must have gone over well," Stephen said with a knowing smile.

"She went, didn't she? I suppose I will hear about it plenty, later."

"I could just about guarantee it. I'm surprised Benton went for it. What did you two do, outfox him?"

"Not at all, Stephen Brown. I am insulted you would think such a thing. He was happy to have Carrie go along. He made some comment about not being able to deal with hysterical old maids."

Stephen laughed. "Poor Benton. He needs a few lessons in political correctness. Which I'm sure he got from Carrie."

"Needs lessons in more than that," Hannah muttered. "Carrie, for some reason has decided to forgive Benton and has been on me to give him a chance."

"And you?" Stephen asked.

"I have always given him a chance, until I could not stand his ineptness any longer. Maybe he has learned something by now. A person can hope already," Hannah said, rolling her eyes heavenward. "Anyhow, i need to cooperate with the police. We have to work together if I am going to find out who killed Nettie. Don't smile, Stephen, this is not a funny business. This is murder and deadly serious."

"That it is," Stephen agreed. "I never suggested otherwise."

"Why is it people smile at me like I am cute, but not very bright? They look at me like I am not to be taken serious, only tolerated. Why? I do not like that, not at all," Hannah said, her voice rising like steam from a kettle. She knew she was being testy, but she couldn't help it. She supposed Nettie's murder was excuse enough for her irritation.

She stood up from where she had been perched on the edge of the couch and begin pacing.

Stephen looked like he wished he was back in his hardware store out of harm's and Hannah's way. He didn't answer her rhetorical question.

Hannah wasn't about to let him off that easily. She turned to look at him seated in front of her. Standing, she was about eye level with him. "Well?"

"Hannah, how many Amish grandmothers run around the countryside involving themselves in murder and other major crimes? You could sit home and make tons of money with your quilt orders. People would kill for one of your quilts...oops, not a good phrase to use now, is it?" Stephen said, looking thoroughly chagrined. Hannah glared silently at him.

"I mean," he continued, "you are famous in this part of the country for your quilts. Playing detective is the last thing people expect to see someone like you doing. You're an anomaly, Granny."

Hannah looked at him less sternly. Poor fella, he stumbled on her at a bad time. He was easy to look at for an Englisher; Carrie had good taste. Stephen's thick brown hair tumbled onto a broad forehead, and framed large hazel eyes. He was tall and lean and despite being well into his thirties possessed a boyish earnestness. The total package that was Stephen Brown has proved irresistible to many juries.

Not long after Carrie and Molly came back into his life, he'd given up practicing contingency law, to take over his father's Crossroads Hardware store in the small, heavily Amish hamlet of Farmers Corners. Caroline didn't particularly approve of the specialty of contingency law which some people referred to as "ambulance chasing", so Hannah figured Stephen had now come up a notch or two in her granddaughter's estimation. According to Carrie, he still had a way to go.

"I am in a foul mood, Stephen Brown. Do not take any mind of me. I am upset over Nettie and need a night's sleep before I can decide where to start figuring out who killed her. Before that, I have Jen to face."

"I'll grab Molly's robe and get out of here, Hannah. You don't need me here with everything else that's going on. Unless you want some company?"

"So I can vent my frustration on you? You are a good soul, Stephen Brown. Get the robe and go."

Stephen hadn't been gone more than five minutes when Hannah heard Caroline's key in the lock.

Caroline flopped into the nearest chair and kicked off her shoes. Then she told Hannah about the visit to the Shoop farm.

"So, what are we to think?" Hannah asked. "That some killer is roaming around the countryside?"

"Benton thinks so. He's called in the State Police to help his men begin a search first thing in the morning," Caroline answered.

"And he's given up on the idea that Nettie knew her assailant?"

"Apparently so, Gran. Your theory made sense to me. But how do we explain the man Sadie and Annie saw? The footprints sure make it look like the same guy who was at Nettie's."

"What if this fellow was not involved with the murder, excepting that he stumbled on it like I did?" Hannah said.

"That's kinda farfetched, Gran. Who would be wandering around the countryside? And why? And if he did find Nettie's body, why wouldn't he call the police?"

"Cause they would think he was the killer, that is why."

"They think that, anyway. No, this time I think there's no mystery about who the killer is. It's our big footed man. All they have to do is find him."

"Should not be too hard. There are no miles of cornfield to hide in. Most of the field are fallow. The police will search every building. They will turn him up." Hannah had a lot more faith in the State Police's ability to come up with the man than she did in Benton's.

"I think I heard a car pull up. I bet it's Jen, Gran," Caroline said, going to the window and looking out towards the front. "It is Jennet, and she's not alone. There's a tall man with her."

CHAPTER EIGHT

Caroline opened the door to a pale, but composed Jennet Hope, and a handsome, distinguished looking man who looked very familiar.

Jen gave Caroline the briefest of hugs as Caroline ushered the two into the small entryway where Hannah waited. The minute Jen saw the older woman, she began to cry quietly.

"Granny," Jen said, sniffing slightly into a linen handkerchief. Her companion stood quietly to one side as Hannah stretched up to put her arms around Jen.

"Ian Hunter," the man said quietly to Caroline.

"Ah, yes," Caroline said, remembering where she'd seen him. "BBC Financial Correspondent?" She'd seen his reports on American television many times.

"Until two months ago. I'm working at NBC now," he answered in a British accent as smooth as brandied cream. "Didn't think Jennet should drive down here alone. A death is a shock no one should bear alone. It's a double blow to lose one's twin and under such circumstances."

"Oh, I'm sorry. I haven't introduced Ian," Jennet said.

Caroline watched amused as Ian's charm worked on Hannah. Her normally unflappable grandmother tittered like a schoolgirl as Ian patted her extended hand. "I've heard wonderful things about you, Mrs. Miller."

"Everyone calls me Hannah or Granny Hanny," she said, laughing girlishly. "We Amish do not make much of titles such as misses, mister or doctor. We seem like a strange bunch until you get used to us."

"I'm looking forward to the pleasure," Ian answered. "So far, I'm fascinated."

Boy is he suave, Caroline thought. She'd never seen Granny quite so charmed by an Englisher. Of course this guy was an <u>authentic</u> Englisher; that accent combined with gorgeous looks and perfect manners was an irresistible combination.

As Caroline busied herself getting coffee in the semi- open kitchen,, she had ample opportunity to study both Jennet and Ian.

Jennet was even more striking in person than she was on television. The contrast between her shining, blunt-cut dark hair, and satiny, flawless complexion was highlighted by the severity of her black wool jumpsuit. At age 45, Jennet didn't have a single line or mark in her face. She looked as young as Caroline at 30. Caroline knew Jennet's personal fountain of youth was located in the clinic of a Fifth Avenue plastic surgeon. Hannah had told her the story of how Jennet had undergone a face lift, and when Nettie had seen the results, she wanted one, too, despite her fear of pain. According to Jennet, it was a pretty painless procedure, but Nettie needed more tranquilizers and painkillers than Jen did to get her through the surgery. At the moment, Jennet's flawless face was marred only by red rimmed eyes.

Ian Hunter was sitting on the love-seat next to Jennet. His cobalt-blue eyes studied her face intently and responded to every nuance in her expression. When she looked troubled, it was Ian's brow that furrowed. He had his handkerchief in her hand before tears barely had time more than to well in her large blue eyes. There is a man who has it bad, and a woman who doesn't know how lucky she is, Caroline observed. Jennet seemed too involved in her own sorrow to notice Ian at all.

Granny had been telling Jennet about the progress of the case, including the latest developments at the Shoops.

"Thank you for letting Jennet stay with you, Caroline," Ian said. "She'll be protected from the intrusion of the press. They can be quite unmerciful where a story like this is concerned." Ian spoke as if he was not a member of the very same profession.

"You are welcome as well, Ian, if you don't mind staying in my little girl's room. She's at her father's this weekend."

Caroline wasn't too concerned about where Ian slept, in Molly's room, or with Jen in the guest room, but Granny was very straitlaced about such things, and Caroline respected her values. Besides, despite Ian's obvious devotion to Jen, Caroline had no idea if they had an intimate physical relationship, or just an emotional connection.

"Thank you, Caroline, I'd appreciate that. I do want to stay near Jennet in case she needs anything. Dealing with the police can be quite a nasty business, indeed."

Caroline hoped Granny wouldn't suggest she, too, stay the night as well. She would have to sleep with Caroline and Caroline knew what that would be like. Hannah slept four hours a night. Then she would be up stalking around like an energetic panther. Normally Hannah passed the extra nighttime hours working on her quilts or reading mysteries, but with the stimulation of Nettie's murder on her mind, she would want to talk. And Caroline hadn't inherited her ability to function on such a small amount of sleep.

"I'll run you home now, Granny," Caroline suggested after the suitcases had been brought in. "I'm sure Jen is exhausted. Tomorrow won't be an easy day for any of us."

"Please allow me take you home, Hannah," Ian said. "If you show me the way, I shouldn't have any trouble finding my way back alone."

Caroline didn't have time to decline his offer before Hannah spoke up. "I was hoping you would volunteer," she said guilelessly. "You are the first real British Englisher I have met."

Jen and Caroline smiled at Hannah's complete lack of pretension. Caroline thought Granny's directness must be especially refreshing to Jennet and Ian considering the kind of world they customarily dealt with.

Caroline wondered how captivated Ian would be by Hannah's directness while driving her home. After the better part of an hour in Hannah's company, he would probably be glad to escape. Caroline could imagine the inquisition now. Ian would be asked, and probably answer, questions about every facet of his life, including how much money he made and if he dyed his hair. Hannah had no shame; she would ask anyone anything. What always surprised Caroline was that people would tell Hannah whatever she wanted to know. Caroline often thought if her grandmother hadn't been born Amish, she would have made a first rate trial lawyer.

After Hannah and Ian had gone, Caroline turned to Jen, who was sitting with her feet tucked under her and staring at the embers of the fire.

"I'll put on another log, Jen, or would you like to go to bed?"

"I don't think I could sleep yet, Carrie. I don't want to be alone. Would you sit here with me?"

"Of course," Caroline answered, and after refilling the coffee cups and putting a fresh log on the fire, sat at the opposite end of the couch. Stirring her coffee, she waited for Jen to talk if she wanted to.

40

Jennet stared into the fire and finally began speaking in a dreamy voice. "I always thought I would be the first to die, not Nettie. She was so careful - never took any physical chances. She was too afraid of getting hurt. Nettie hated pain." Jennet took a sip of her coffee. A piece of the log broke off and the flames blazed higher. "I teased her when she married Peter. I said it was because he was a dentist and could manage to take such good care of her teeth that she'd never have to get a filling." Jen smiled weakly. "She wouldn't even get her ears pierced. And then to die such a horrible and probably painful death." Jennet buried her face in her hands and began to sob.

Caroline moved over and put her arms around the older woman. "She probably didn't suffer much," she murmured, hoping it was true. She knew there wasn't much else she could say; Jennet would have to find the inner strength to pull herself through her grief. All Caroline could do was to be there.

"I suppose I'll never really get over this, Carrie, but I can't just fall to pieces." Jennet took a shuddering breath and blew her nose on the handkerchief Ian had left with her.. "It will be easier to put this behind me after the police catch the killer. It sounds like they've almost got him. It shouldn't take too long. Maybe by tomorrow?" Jennet looked at Caroline questioningly. Jennet knew as well as Caroline the killer was either caught or loose; there was no 'almost' about it.

"We can hope," Caroline answered. "We can only hope."

By noon of the following day, despite an intensive search, there was no sign of the killer. Every farmhouse, shed, and copse of trees within range of a man on foot had been checked. Nothing. He had vanished.

"It means this guy has to have wheels," Benton said, sitting at Caroline's kitchen table. "He could be anywhere. Probably miles from here. But don't you worry; we have an A.P.B. out. The Shoop ladies' description is kind of sparse so we borrowed an artist from State Police and he's out there now trying to put together a sketch."

Jennet looked wan despite the addition of a bright blue scarf at the throat of her charcoal gray dress. Deep shadows circled her eyes. She obviously hadn't slept well, but she looked composed, and strikingly beautiful. Her beauty and celebrity were not lost on Benton.

He sat ramrod straight, dressed in a white shirt and dark blue suit, cut a bit too tightly across the shoulders. He was obviously carefully dressed for meeting the famous Jennet Hope. His sartorial elegance was spoiled somewhat by a small grease spot on his yellow tie. Ian's presence was a surprise to the policeman, and Caroline noticed that whenever Benton could take his eyes off Jennet, he sneaked furtive glances at the impeccably dressed newsman. Ian, looked like he just stepped off a magazine cover, wore a deep red cashmere polo shirt and gray wool slacks atop well-polished, tasseled loafers.

Jennet got right to what concerned her most, the release of Nettie's body. "When will we be able to hold the services, Chief?"

Only Jennet's elegant hands betrayed her emotions; a sapphire ring glittered as she tightly clutched a lace edged handkerchief.

"The coroner will be releasing the deceased to the funeral home today, Ma'am," Benton answered. "You can go right on ahead with the plans. My men are almost through with the house. I figure by tomorrow, it'll be okay to get in there, if you …need anything for the deceased to, uh, wear."

Jennet shuddered. "Oh, I couldn't…"

"It's all right, my dear," Ian broke in. "I'm sure Hannah or Caroline and I can get whatever is needed." He patted Jennet's hand.

Benton had only perfunctorily questioned Jennet. In Caroline's opinion, he was deferential to a fault. Other than to ask her whereabouts when Nettie was killed, he hadn't asked another pertinent question. The case was still wide open, but Benton was proceeding as if it was already wrapped up and put to bed.

The mystery man could be anyone; there was as yet nothing to connect him directly with Nettie's murder. Caroline thought of at least a dozen questions Benton should be asking. Hannah had probably thought of a dozen more. To begin with, Benton should ask Jennet who had a key to the house. Jennet often spent time with Nettie, and would be familiar with her sister's routine and other intimate details of her life. Then he should ask Jennet who might want to harm Nettie. The more Caroline thought of Benton sitting there fawning over Jennet because she was famous, the more irked she became.

Then she remembered she was going to give him a chance to do it his way. Maybe he was only waiting until Jennet recovered her equilibrium. Jennet, who was leaning on Ian's shoulder, still looked pretty fragile. Nevertheless Benton's job was to get information, despite the distress of informants. Death was always distressing to those close to the victim. Caroline was annoyed he was approaching Jennet so timorously. There are ways of gently eliciting facts. Avoiding questioning was not one of them. He'd never find out a damn thing this way. Still, she'd wouldn't butt in with questioning Jennet - yet.

"Chief Benton," Caroline said, "Any news on the footprints?"

"Our township has only limited facilities," Benton answered, for Jen and Ian's benefit. "We utilize the services of the state crime lab for technical work. Since it's the weekend, we probably won't hear anything until Monday. By then we'll have the man and the shoes that made those prints." Benton smiled smugly.

Caroline stopped herself from saying what she was thinking. Yeah, I'll believe it when I see it. You were going to have him by morning, too. Benton was so anxious to get rid of a murder case, he was jumping at the obvious conclusion whether or not the facts warranted it. As with Joshua's case, Benton was looking for the easy way out.

Despite the fact she was appalled at the way Benton was handling the case, she wouldn't say anything else to Benton now. She was going to save that pleasure for Hannah.

Caroline knew Hannah was already to plunge into the case. When she heard how remiss Benton was in questioning Jen, she'd really want to leap into the fray. Caroline wouldn't be able to hold her back, even if she wanted to. Looking at Benton doing little else but posturing for Jennet's benefit, Caroline knew she wasn't going to stop Granny. Someone had to care.

CHAPTER NINE

Hannah waited impatiently for Daniel to finish his chores in the dairy so he could drop her by Carrie's house. Would nothing hurry the fellow? She knew the answer to that only too well. Nothing ever hurried her methodical son. He would take her when he was ready, good and ready, on his regular Saturday trip to town, and not before. If only Rebecca, her daughter-in-law, who served as the local midwife, wasn't using the small buggy out attending a birth at the Lapp place, Hannah would have driven herself in.

Hannah walked around her grossdotti, or granddaddy, house as it was called in English. It was a smaller house attached by a common porch to the main house where her son Daniel lived with his wife and their two children, eighteen-year old Joshua and ten-year old Bethany. The grossdotti house had been built twelve years ago for Hannah and her late husband when he retired from the dairy farm. Amish elders were never relegated to "old folks homes", as Hannah called retirement homes, but lived near the family and took part in running the farms and helping in the home as much as they wanted and were able to.

Non-Amish people were surprised to find an elderly Amish widow living in an ultra modern house, complete with great room and plate glass windows. Hannah knew as long as she didn't use electricity, there were no proscriptions against any kind of architecture one wanted. She wanted lots of large expanses of white wall to display her famous quilts. More importantly, she needed all the light she could get to illuminate her work, both in when progress and completed.

Hannah Miller was one of the better known quilt makers in the county. Her hand crafted quilts were much in demand, and she had orders enough to keep her busy for two years ahead. With a family the size of hers, she made many of her quilts for weddings and new babies. Hannah's designs were not always traditional; her most recent work, still on the frame, depicted Lancaster County's hot air balloons worked in brilliant colors. Although nothing in her religion prohibited subject matter in quilts, Hannah herself turned down several orders she felt a bit too bizarre. She said she had to look at a quilt while she was making it, and she was not going to accept a commission for a quilt featuring Elvis portraits.

The quilt she had made for Nettie, the one she had tried to deliver yesterday when she found the body, sat on the table. The police had kept the wrapping, but let Hannah take the quilt. What was going to become of Nettie's quilt now? It was paid for. Hannah wasn't sure who would inherit, Jen or Kaitlin. She would find out soon enough; Carrie's law firm represented the Adams family, and Caroline had written Nettie's will after Bob disappeared. Nettie hadn't mentioned anything about it to Hannah, and, of course, it was privileged information. Hannah wouldn't ask Carrie. She'd find out soon enough.

Whoever inherits had a good motive. Between the business and the house, despite Bob Adams cleaning out the bank account, Nettie was a wealthy woman. But so was Jennet, Money wouldn't be a motive for her.

Though she found it hard to believe Jen could have had anything to do with her sister's murder, Hannah wasn't ready to eliminate any suspects. Her own feelings had to be put aside. Her goal was to find Nettie's murderer. No matter how many big strangers the Shoop sisters saw or how many footprints were around, and despite what Benton assumed, Hannah was going to proceed as if this were a regular investigation.

Benton and his intruder theory aside, Hannah knew Nettie. Never would she open the door for a stranger, nor de-activate the alarm when she was alone inside the house.

Hannah had learned to listen to her intuition. It told her Nettie Adams knew her killer. The police said there was no sign of forced entry. Hannah herself saw the body, long enough to know one thing; Nettie hadn't been sexually attacked. Even if she had opened the door to someone, Nettie's body was found upstairs. Nettie never would have taken a stranger upstairs. Nothing was out of place on the first floor. If she was trying to escape from someone, she would have run out one of the four doors downstairs, not gone to the second floor to be trapped and murdered. No sir, no stranger killed Nettie.

Benton seemed to have all but abandoned any theory but that of an intruder. It was going to be up to Hannah and Caroline. Hannah couldn't explain the footprints - yet. She would work in the manner of those successful sleuths who populated the books she read. The footprints would be explained when she found the killer in the usual way — by dogged attention to detail and good detective work.

She wanted to be there when Benton questioned Jennet Hope. Despite questioning Ian pretty thoroughly last night on the way back to the farm, Hannah wanted to hear what Jennet would say to Benton, and ask a few questions herself. Ian seemed to answer Hannah's questions honestly. She had no doubt that anyone as skilled in interviewing techniques as he was unaware he was being grilled. But he hadn't mentioned it, nor did he seem to dissemble in his answers. If what Ian said was accurate, it had taken him less than four hours to drive from New York. That meant Jennet could have easily driven back with time to spare between the time Hannah discovered Nettie's body and the time she called them. And she could have flown, whether in a private plane or commercially, in even less time. Ian did confirm that Jennet was in New York, but could one assume he wasn't an accomplice, or providing Jennet with an alibi? To be sure Hannah would confirm someone else besides Ian saw Jennet in New York. Ian wouldn't be the first man to be suckered in by a beautiful face. And Hannah herself wouldn't want to be the first old Amish woman to be suckered in by a handsome face and an English accent. She would double-check Jennet's alibi.

Hannah had filled several pages of a loose-leaf notebook with things to do and people to check concerning the case. Sleeping four hours a night gave her lots of thinking time. Good thing; solving Nettie's murder wasn't going to be easy.

By the time Hannah arrived at Caroline's house, Benton was long gone, and Jen and Ian were at the funeral home making arrangements for Nettie's memorial services.

"Don't know why you are surprised, Carrie, that Kiel Benton was too awed by Jennet to ask her any questions. He was thrilled with the very idea of meeting her," Hannah commented. "She is very pretty."

"I noticed."

"All this runching around the countryside by the police is not doing any good. Besides, Benton is barking up the wrong tree... I know, you don't like the way I talk in clichés," Hannah said, catching the furrow in Caroline's brow. "Why not? It makes my point clearer. Now if I were Miss Agatha Cristie or Miss Anne Perry, and writing a book, I would watch myself. Since I am not, I will talk my way. You are welcome to talk yours."

"Thanks, you are too kind." Caroline smiled.

"I know; some things cannot be helped. Now if we are through improving my syntax, let us get cracking on this case," Hannah said, opening her notebook.

Thirty minutes later, twice as many written pages from the notebook were scattered on the table. The two women laid out a to-do list several pages long.

"Granny, you realize I have to get back to my other life come Monday. I have to go to work and Molly will be home."

"Ooh, yes. Molly. I forgot to tell you Stephen dropped by last night when you were out at the Shoops with Benton."

"Why?"

"To get Molly's robe. So he said. I think he wanted to see you."

"He's supposed to call; we have an agreement on that. He's not Amish, despite that silly pseudo Amish farm he has. He has no excuse for not using a phone. He has phones all over the place out of sight," Caroline said, briskly stacking note book pages.

"He tried to call, but we had the phone tied up. Remember?"

"Okay. So?"

"He said Molly could stay out there as long as you are needed; his housekeeper can take Molly to school on Monday."

"After he drops by again for Molly's clothes?"

"Well, I would have given him some last night, but how was I to know what a little English girl needs for school. I don't know much about Beauty and the Beast lunch pails or Lion King sweatshirts."

"Oh, no; of course not. But you know an awful lot about matchmaking, you old reprobate you," Caroline said, laughing. "Ease up, Granny. Stephen is growing on me, although I shouldn't tell you that. You're incorrigible enough now."

"All right. I know when I am not wanted. By the way, Stephen said he would be glad to help if he could," Hannah said with a twinkle in her eye. Carrie would come around where Stephen was concerned. Eventually. She had a definite streak of stubbornness; must have come from her grandfather's side.

"I told Jennet and Ian we might be out for a few hours this afternoon. I had a feeling you'd want to get right on this. I think they'll be glad of the peace and quiet."

"I am glad you offered to let them stay here, Carrie. The papers I saw on the way in are full of the story. Jen would not get much rest at a hotel."

"I only hope none of the media finds out they're here. But I guess Ian could handle it; he's one of them."

They divided up the list. Caroline had friends from her days at a New York law firm, and with a few phone calls could easily check on Jennet's alibi and, if necessary, air schedules, rentals of private planes and car rental company records. Hannah would question Jennet, not only about her relationship with her sister, but to find out what she knew about Peter Drew, Nettie's ex-husband, and their daughter, Kaitlin. Then together Hannah and Caroline planned to visit Peter and Kaitlin.

The police had already questioned the neighbors in their search for the prowler. Hannah suspected the questioning was pretty perfunctory, if it followed Benton's usual pattern. Wouldn't hurt to talk to people at a bit more length. Folks, particularly Amish, were more inclined to talk to Hannah than to a stranger, specially when the stranger was an English policeman. Especially when the subject was murder.

CHAPTER TEN

It only took a few minutes for Caroline to call her old friend, Jimbo Johnson, an investigator she had worked with when she practiced in New York. He promised to start checking right away on Jen. With Jimbo's contacts, she didn't expect it to take too long to learn what they wanted to know.

Hannah tried to call Dr. Peter Drew with no success at either his home or his office. Both phones were picked up by a machine. The best she could do was to leave a message and tell Peter they'd like to drop by his home later.

They knew where Kaitlin worked, but not where she lived. "We'll have to go by the store where she works and see if they'll give out her home address," Caroline said. "I think, as her mother's attorney, I should be able to talk the manager into it."

A short time later, they were at Lancaster's largest mall, Park City Mall.

It took Caroline some minutes of circling around the crowded parking lot before she found a place.

"It is not so much trouble in a carriage," Hannah remarked, getting out of the car.

"With a carriage you'd still be on your way here," Caroline answered, as they made their way through hordes of Saturday shoppers.

"Carrie, that is terrible; Christmas decorations up already. And it is still October yet," Hannah yelled at Caroline in order to be heard through the din of canned music and voices.

Disc Den was a narrow slice of a store in which customers had to pass through sensors to enter or leave. Hannah, who spent little time in malls, was fascinated with the display of plastic cosseted compact discs.

"What is reggae?" she asked. "Why do they call these plastic cases 'jewel boxes?' A person can hardly keep up with this English world. I just recently got rap figured out."

Caroline didn't answer. She had less time than her grandmother to keep up with music trends. "Do you know Kate when you see her, Granny?"

Caroline had spotted a young woman who bore such a striking resemblance to the Hope sisters, there was no question as to her identity. She had to be Kaitlin Drew.

"See, Granny, over there back of the register? Is that Kate?" She indicated a girl with brassy-red, shoulder-length hair laughing with another employee.

"Oh, my, it is Kate...working here with her mother not buried yet." Hannah sounded as distressed as she felt. Such a thing would never happen in an Amish family, and compounding her shock was the realization that Nettie and her daughter must have been estranged even beyond death.

As Hannah approached the register, Kate came out from behind the counter. She was tall, perhaps 5' 9" or so, and despite the obviously dyed hair, and unbecoming, harsh make-up, strikingly pretty. Dressed in well-worn, very tight jeans, with a white tee shirt under a shiny leather vest, there was nothing to distinguish her from the customers except a store badge with her name.

"Hi, Granny Hanny," she said as casually as if it was a normal situation and Hannah was a usual customer.

As usual Hannah was direct. "My granddaughter, Carrie here, and I have come here to talk to you, Kaitlin."

"Fine," the girl shrugged. "I have a fifteen minute break coming up. There's only one quiet place in the mall to talk, Dounne's restaurant, right around the corner. I'll see you there in five minutes."

Hannah and Caroline found the restaurant almost deserted. It was too elegant and expensive to appeal to families out for a day of shopping, and it was too early in the afternoon to draw any dinner traffic.

"You suppose Kaitlin hasn't heard about her mother?" Caroline asked.

"Not likely, Carrie. It's all over the news. People are talking about it everywhere. Even the Amish would know about such a thing. No, Kate knows; she just does not care," Hannah said, idly examining the silver for spots. In Hannah's experience, the dimmer the light, the more likely a person was to find smudged silver.

"I remember you telling Chief Benton that Kaitlin said in court she hated her mother."

"I figured that was mostly teen-age dramatics. I had no idea how much Kate really hated Nettie. Guess I know now."

"Shh, here she comes," Caroline cautioned.

They went through the motions of ordering, but as soon as they were served, Hannah plunged right in.

"We are all sorry about your mother's death, Kaitlin dear."

"I know you are, Granny Hanny," the girl answered, her voice level, and without a flicker of emotion showing on her face. She turned to Caroline. "I hear you're a lawyer now, Carrie. Was it hard to leave the Amish?"

"Yes, it was hard, Kaitlin. Very hard."

Hannah wondered if Kaitlin felt some empathy with Carrie. In a way, Kate, too, had left her people. But unlike Carrie, Kate had not made peace with her decision. Now with her mother murdered, could she ever?

"We are here to ask you some questions, Kate," Hannah began. "We are trying to help the police find the person who murdered your mother. I am sure you would like to help."

The girl shrugged, her eyes downcast. "I suppose, but what can I do? I was on the outs with her. You know, totally estranged."

"How long has it been since you've seen your mother?"

"Four years, about."

"Why didn't you want to live with her and Bob?"

"I, uh, felt like I was in the way. They didn't want me around," Kate still hadn't looked Hannah directly in the eye. Either she was embarrassed or she was withholding information.

"Then why did your mother fight for your custody?"

"Because Daddy wanted me; she was selfish."

"How did you get along with Bob Adams?" Hannah asked.

"He was all right," Kate answered in a small voice.

"Did you like him then?" Hannah pressed.

"I don't remember." Kate's voice fell off even further. She swirled her tea bag around so hard that the hot liquid splashed on her hand. She didn't seem to notice as the tea dribbled down her hand and dropped onto the tablecloth.

"I mean, he was away lots, working on some construction project upstate. When he was home, the two of them were off by themselves. I barely knew him," Kate said more strongly. "Do you think he killed her?"

"The police do not know who killed your mother, Kate."

"The paper said they were looking for some guy seen in the area."

So she had read the paper. Not surprising, Hannah thought.

"It was not Bob Adams. It was a stranger; he was seen by neighbors. At the moment, there is nothing to connect him directly with your mother's death."

"So, you're out questioning everyone who had anything against her. Including me." Kaitlin looked at Hannah for the first time, her eyes icy blue.

"Wouldn't you, if you wanted to find the person responsible?" Caroline asked.

"Yeah, I guess," the girl answered. "I hated her, but I don't kill people. I was at my dad's house all yesterday morning. He can tell you." Kate reached into her pocket and plunked a handful of change on the table. "I gotta go back to work," she said, standing.

"Kate, your Aunt Jennet is here. She would like to see you, I know. Where can we reach you?" Hannah asked, standing to look up at the girl.

"Dad knows how to get a hold of me. But, Granny Hanny," Kaitlin said as she turned to go. "I don't want to see Jennet. She reminds me too much of my mother."

"Well, Carrie, what do you think about Kate already?" Hannah asked, after she and Caroline were back in the car.

"Besides the fact she's not telling us anything? Besides the fact she also hated Bob Adams? Besides the fact she's an emotional wreck? Did you see her nails? They were bitten to the quick."

"Yah, besides all that. Why all the hate? Either this girl is lying and has plenty of reason to detest her mother and Bob, or she is disturbed. Either way, she better have an alibi because she sure has some kind of motive."

"You thinking what I am?" Caroline asked.

"Probably. I do not know if it is only a sign of the times that the first thing to pop into my mind is child abuse. Or is that a logical thing to think Kate is hiding?" Hannah asked, sadly.

"Both. It's exactly what I thought. She shows all the classic signs — anger, nervousness, secrecy, faulty memory. She really may not be able to remember what happened or why she hates her mother."

"This kind of thing is a heavy burden to lay at the foot of Nettie's grave," Hannah sighed. "I have a feeling Peter can help us find out if it is true."

"If he knows, he hasn't been able to help Kate much in the last four years. She is a young woman who is full of contradictory emotions. Let's hope she really does have an alibi because if what we suspect is true, I agree with you. Kaitlin Drew has one strong motive."

CHAPTER ELEVEN

"You should invest in one of those cellular phones, Carrie. All the newest detectives have them," Hannah said, as they got into Caroline's car.

"For the umpteenth time, Granny, I am not a detective. You may fancy yourself one; I am an attorney, nothing more. I do not need to have a cell phone glued to my ear day and night."

"Isn't the expression 24/7?" Hannah asked. "Don't all the really successful attorneys have those phones?" Hannah asked, still hopeful.

"Only the compulsive ones, Granny. Guess I'll have to settle for semi-successful. Sorry."

"It would help if you had one. Now how am I supposed to call Peter?"

"You could pretend you are Amish and simply drop by his house," Caroline answered as she headed towards Ephrata where Dr. Peter Drew lived.

"Sarcasm doesn't become you, Dear," Hannah answered.

As usual, Granny thinks I've really gone over the wall, Caroline thought. Since I left the Amish, I should be more English than the English…have every gadget ever invented. And all available for her convenience.

They pulled up in front of the very elegant home of Peter Drew. Wow, Caroline thought, dentistry must be even more profitable than I imagined. The house, a rambling redwood ranch affair which looked more like California Carmel than Pennsylvania Dutch, sat behind protective wooden fencing and come evening would be additionally secured by visible perimeter lighting. Now, it glowed benignly in the autumn sunlight.

Hannah extracted herself from the seat belt. "These belts wouldn't be a bad idea in our carriages. Might save us from a few tumbles when we get hit by one of those manic English drivers," she observed. "Think I'll suggest it to the bishop. Then, just maybe in a few years, they might go for the idea." Hannah was sometimes impatient with the resistance of the Amish bishops to changes.

Caroline knew better than to get into a discussion with her grandmother. "Uh-hmm", Caroline said noncommittal. "It's hard to tell if anyone is home."

Hannah didn't answer, but strode towards the front door, a carved wooden affair, and rang the bell.

A disembodied male voice floated out from a well concealed grill near the door. "Who's there?"

"It is Hannah Miller, Peter. I would like to see you please."

Several seconds later a man opened the door. He looked familiar to Caroline. She must have seen Peter Drew somewhere along the line, but it would had been back when she was still Amish and not noticing English men, especially ones old enough to be her father. He was probably just another customer at the Crossroads Hardware where she worked then. Peter was very tall, maybe 6'5", and even at nearly fifty, looked as gangly as a teenager. At the moment, he also looked harried. His face wore a stubble of graying beard and his thinning brown hair was in need of combing or stroubbly, as Hannah would say. He looked like he'd been up all night thinking about something important.

"The newspapers have been bugging me since yesterday. Guess they finally gave up," Peter said, looking around. "Come in."

After Caroline had been introduced, and she and Hannah were seated with soft drinks in Peter's spacious living room. Hannah dug a pencil out of her commodious black handbag and began idly playing with it. Caroline gave her a quizzical look. It wasn't like Hannah to display nervous behavior. Caroline guessed her grandmother was up to something.

"You are all right, Peter?" Hannah began.

"Yeah, fine. Thanks for trying to call me, Hannah, before the papers sprung it on me. I don't know what they want from me. I haven't seen Nettie for four years. I can't tell 'em anything."

"It's big news around here," Caroline commented. "The biggest story since Joshua was on trial last summer. The media is like a pack of jackals scarfing up everything."

"Poor Nettie. It's a hell of a way to die," Peter answered. "For anybody. The news says the cops are looking for some prowler."

"They are. As of an hour ago, they had not found him. He seems to have vanished," Hannah said. Suddenly the pencil flipped out of her hand. She quickly retrieved it from under Peter's foot and put it back into her bag.

"Peter," she continued. "Do you mind if Carrie and I ask you some questions about Nettie?"

"Go ahead."

"Do know if she had any enemies?"

"Hah!" Peter said. "Not our Nettie; she was sweet as sugar, the nicest gal around."

"I suppose you have plenty of reason to be bitter."

"Thanks to Nettie, my business fell off by half. I've built it up again, no thanks to Queen Annette. Now I don't dare even order a soft drink in public; somebody might think I'm hitting the bottle. Funny, people like their dentists to have steady hands." Peter lifted his glass, shaking it dramatically as the ice tinkled piercingly in the quiet room.

"We went to see Kaitlin, Peter," Hannah said.

"Good," Peter said. "I tried to call her, but she doesn't answer her phone, and hasn't returned my calls to her at work. I even went over to that dump she lives in, but she wasn't there. I didn't want her to find out from the newspapers, but guess she did," he said, running his hand through his already mussed hair. "I didn't think she'd be too upset, but just the same, Nettie was her mother..."

"Kate seemed fine when we saw her. I sort of got the idea she is a girl who keeps things inside - does not share her feelings."

"She doesn't share them with me, Hannah. Sometimes I think the only reason she wanted to live with me was so she didn't have to live with her mother and Bob Adams."

"How did she get along with Bob?" Caroline asked.

"I don't know; she hardly ever mentioned him. Only thing she ever said about him was in reference to her mother. Kate's main gripe was that Nettie ignored her whenever Bob was around and fought with her whenever he wasn't."

"All teenagers go through a period of not getting along with their parents, especially with the same-sex parent."

"All teenagers don't say their mothers abused them," Peter answered.

"What?" Hannah and Caroline said in unison.

"Oh, I don't mean physically," Peter answered. "Nettie was emotionally abusive to Kate. Jealous, I guess. Stupid, isn't it? As beautiful as Nettie…was. Kate said Nettie beat her down verbally at every turn; it was worse when Bob was around. And he didn't do a thing to nip it in the bud. Kate said he laughed loudest at the mean little jokes Nettie made at Kate's expense."

"What kind of jokes?" Caroline asked.

"Petty stuff, like commenting on Kate's skin. 'Kaitlin, I'm afraid you're going to have a bad skin problem…it's starting already.' That kind of bull. You know how touchy kids are."

"Poor Kate and poor Nettie," Hannah said. "I had no idea Nettie was so cruel. I knew she was impatient, but treating your own daughter like that is …" Hannah shook her head sadly.

"I had to get Kate out of that house," Peter said. "When she was first here, things were okay for a couple of years, but then she got in with a wild bunch of kids. Her grades went down the tubes and she started talking about dropping out of school. I tightened up and got stricter…should have known better."

"Yah, the tighter you pull the reins, the balkier the horse," Hannah said, with the voice of experience.

"I should have followed the Amish way of giving her more freedom at that age. Of course Amish teenagers don't get pregnant and into drugs. Not that Kate did, but I could see it coming," Peter said.

"Amish kids do not get into bad trouble very often only because when we only give them freedom when they know responsibility goes along with it. A lot of English teens aren't taught to think ahead. But, Peter, you must be getting along with Kate since she said she was here yesterday morning."

"That's right, Hannah, she was. I guess Kate and I gave each other alibis. Kate wanted to stop by and go through some clothes she left here when she moved in with that creep."

"Kate has a boyfriend?" Hannah asked.

"Chris Locke."

The way Peter spat out the words told Hannah she need not ask his opinion of Kate's boyfriend. "She met him at school?"

"Yeah. He was a big jock, football player, when Kate was a cheerleader. That was before he got busted for selling drugs and spent some time in the county jail. Even after he dropped out of school, Kate stuck with him. Can't say she isn't loyal to her friends," Peter said, looking disgusted. "Even if she lets herself get dragged down with 'em,"

"What does this Chris Locke look like, Peter?" Hannah asked.

"Big chunk of a kid. My height but a lot heavier. Good teeth though. Looks like somebody saw to it he had orthodontia. I also remember brown hair, too damn long. That's all I ever noticed. Why?"

"Curiosity," said Hannah. "Just curiosity."

"Okay, Samantha Spade, what now?" Caroline asked her grandmother as they drove away from Peter Drew's house. "What did you find out that you didn't know before?"

"For one thing, a lot of men in Lancaster County have big feet...size twelves maybe."

"The reason you dropped the pencil was to get a good look at Peter Drew's feet. Hope he didn't catch on as easily as I did."

"He did not know I was looking."

"And I suppose you think Kate's boyfriend has big feet, too."

"Can you imagine a fella of 6' 5" and big with it, waltzing around on tiny little feet?"

Caroline laughed. "Point well taken, Ms. Spade."

"This isn't a funny business, Carrie. We're after a murderer."

"I'm not laughing, Granny, but you're the one who keeps telling me to lighten up...your words exactly as I recall."

"Touché, dear. I suppose I was just thinking of Kate. What a sad thing. If what she told Peter is true, Nettie was not the woman I thought I knew. I realized she was impatient and short tempered, but not evil. To treat your own child in such a way is evil, plain and simple."

"But was Kate telling Peter the truth, or only part of the truth? What was really going on?" Caroline asked. "Besides Kate there is only one person who might be able to give you some insight. Jennet Hope. She knew her twin better than anyone else."

"I think it is time I had a long talk with Jen. There are a lot of things I want to ask her."

"Don't you think it's odd Peter didn't ask about Jen?"

"Maybe he feels like Kate does; Jennet is just like Nettie."

"Not quite, thank God," Caroline said. "Nettie is dead."

CHAPTER TWELVE

When Caroline pulled up in front of her house, three cars were there - Benton's chief's car, Ian's Mercedes, and Stephen's maroon minivan.

"Oh, great. Look who's come to dinner, two of my favorite people, Stephen and el "Ben" Benton. Doesn't anybody call these days?"

"Well, Carrie, if you had a car phone..."

"Granny..."

"Be nice, Dear. As for Benton - remember, we are cooperating with the police now."

"Oh we are? I forgot. And what excuse do you have for Stephen?"

"Umm, he is bringing back Molly's robe maybe?"

"Right, Granny. Come on; let's get this over with. Maybe Ben has caught Bigfoot."

"Doesn't matter if he has. I tell you no prowler killed Nettie," Hannah answered firmly.

"So you say."

Only Benton and Stephen were waiting in Caroline's sunny living room when she and Hannah walked in.

"Ian let us in. He and Jen are resting," Stephen announced. "I saw the note and decided to wait," he said, referring to the note Caroline left for Jen saying she would be back by 4 o'clock. "Ben came by a few minutes ago. We were discussing the latest on Nettie Adams' murder."

"Hello, Ben," Caroline said. "Something new happen on the case?"

"No sign of the man yet," Benton said wearily. "I came by to tell Miss Hope the coroner has released the deceased to the funeral home. We are done with the Adams house. Miss Hope says you are the deceased's attorney. Right?"

"That's right," Caroline said.

"So, who gets the place?"

"Why do you ask, Chief?"

"Just personal reasons. It's a nice place; I might want to buy it."

Caroline saw Stephen stiffen, and his eyes narrow with quick anger. "And you figure you could help Miss Hope or whoever inherits by taking it off their hands, Chief Benton?" Stephen asked in the prosecutorial tone he had learned in law school.

"Well, a lot of folks wouldn't want a house where a murder happened. I wouldn't have a problem with that. Might take a lot of worry off somebody. Nothing wrong with that." Benton was getting red in the face.

"Of course not," Stephen answered. "At least nothing illegal."

Caroline decided she better put a stop to it before she was refereeing a fight. "Ben, until the will is read, I am not at liberty to divulge its contents. To anyone. Unless you have a subpoena... or you think it has something to do with Nettie's murder."

"Oh, no. We know who murdered Nettie Adams. I just figured..." he stopped, looking first at Stephen, then at Caroline, and finally at Hannah, with a sheepish look.

Quickly Hannah changed the subject. "Tell me, Chief Benton," she said, sounding intrigued. "Do you expect the state crime lab to come up with evidence to link your prowler to the murder?"

Caroline sneaked a look at her grandmother. Hannah knew the answer as well as Benton. "Peace at any price" was the Amish motto, and Hannah was going to use a distraction technique to defuse a confrontation.

"Sure do, Ma'am. We found all kinds of evidence - blood, dirt, fibers. You can bet we will have plenty to link this intruder to the deceased's murder."

"As soon as you find him," Hannah said.

"Oh, we will. We will," Benton answered, although his tone of voice was less confident than his words.

"There is no point to you wasting time here, Chief. I will be happy to relay your message to Jennet. You run along now, unless you are planning to question her?" Hannah asked.

"Don't guess there's any reason to bother Miss Hope," Benton answered, deferentially.

"But you will want to ask her questions later?"

"Oh, sure," Benton answered, not sounding sure at all.

"Good," Hannah said briskly. "Now, I would say you could use some rest, hard as you have been working."

Hannah had effectively dismissed him. As he left, Benton still looked torn between getting away from Stephen, and not wanting to miss seeing Jennet, even if he had no intent of questioning her, at least not until Hannah had mentioned it.

It was all Caroline could do not to smile at her grandmother's wily handling of the chief. One way or another, Jennet would be questioned. Now, if Caroline could only handle Stephen with equal subtlety.

"Thanks, Stephen, for taking Benton on and keeping me from losing it," Caroline said, after Benton had gone.

"Benton is a sloth. He's stupid and lazy," Stephen said.

"Do not insult sloths, Stephen Brown. They may be slow and lazy, but they do not act dishonestly. Chief Benton does," Hannah observed.

"<u>Acting</u> chief, Granny. If I had anything to say about it, he wouldn't be chief. The guy's a slime-ball - trying to get a deal on Nettie's house," Caroline said.

Hannah sat down in Molly's child-size rocker and began rocking back and forth. She looked like an appealing, life-size doll. Caroline saw Stephen smiling fondly at the sight. He and her grandmother had developed a warm relationship. Caroline was beginning to look at Stephen Brown in a new light herself. He had changed from the immature boy who walked out on her before their daughter was born. The man she knew now shouldn't have to pay for his behavior in what was like another life. Catching his eye, Caroline shared the smile with Stephen. He still does have the most amazing amber eyes, she found herself thinking.

The spell was broken by the sound of the rocking chair squeaking on the wooden floor.

"Well, I have decided," Hannah announced.

"Decided what?" Caroline asked.

"I am taking this investigation over from Kiel Benton. Why should I be leading him by the hand? No, sireee, the man is not fit to be chief, and if we help him, he will be."

"I couldn't agree with you more, Granny Hanny," Stephen said. Now what can I do to help you?"

"Plenty, Stephen. I am glad I can count on you. It is going to take a team effort to catch this killer. I know I am counting a lot on my instincts that Nettie was murdered by someone she knew, not some big footed prowler." Hannah rocked harder.

"I, for one," Stephen said, "respect your instincts."

"And I know I can depend on your help, Stephen Brown. If it hadn't been for you, who knows what would have happened to Molly and Bethany that time?" Hannah asked, referring to her last murder case.

"There is something you can do, Stephen," Granny said. "track down that boy friend of Katilin's, the one Peter Drew mentioned. I want to know where he was when Nettie died. If Kaitlin inherits…" Hannah didn't finish her sentence.

"I understand", Stephen said. "I'll get right on it. I have a lot of contacts left from when I was practicing law. If I don't miss my guess, Granny, you already have his name and all the details. Right?"

Hannah nodded. "Most of them. You know I keep notes."

"Like a first rate detective. Our none too bright Benton could learn from you, Granny."

"You are turning into a good assistant, Stephen, well as kind of a nice fellow."

"Come on, you two," Caroline said, smiling. "Enough of the mutual admiration society. There's so much sweetness in here, it could be Valentine's Day instead of Halloween. A girl could get diabetes. What do we do first? Besides question Jennet?"

"Also question Ian. I am curious what Jen may have said to him about Nettie and Kate. He might remember some little something Jen will forget, or not think to tell us," Hannah said. She pulled her notebook from her purse.

"Ian is so besotted with Jen, I doubt if he'd say much if he had any idea Jennet was on the suspect list." Caroline spoke in sotto voice even though Jennet and Ian were at the far end of the house and unlikely to hear her.

"I do not plan to ask him anything about Jennet. Only about what she said. And I will ask in front of her. That Ian Hunter is too smart a cookie to try to pull the wool over his head already," Hannah said.

Caroline saw the corners of Stephen's mouth twitch.

"Granny," Caroline said. "You've got to knock off those clichés, or at least get them right."

"You know what I mean, Carrie. Stop getting me ferdutzed, I mean confused." She consulted her notes. "Then I ask Jennet a long list of questions. Yours, mine and ours." Hannah looked up at Stephen. "You are part of this team now, Stephen. If you think of anything, ask away. I have not forgotten you are a lawyer, too. I need all the expert help I can get. I am only an amateur."

"Yes, Granny Hanny," Stephen said seriously, although Caroline could see his eyes twinkling. "Thank you."

"Next thing," Hannah said. "We get in Nettie's house. My instincts tell me that's where we get some answers already."

CHAPTER THIRTEEN

The memorial service for Annette Adams was set for Tuesday afternoon. Hannah thought it would be a good thing when it was over. Now, having recovered from the initial insulating disbelief of learning of Nettie's death, Jennet's grief was overcoming her. Hannah read enough about twins to know losing one's identical twin was something akin to losing part of oneself. No wonder Jen looked physically ill as well as emotionally drained. Neither of the Hope girls was religious. Doc Hope once told Hannah he was too much of a scientist to go for religious nonsense, and so the girls had grown up without church. That was one thing Hannah couldn't do for them. Amish church was for Amish, even if Doc had allowed the girls to go. Too bad. Jennet could use a strong faith about now. It was a pity some of the English did not have an attitude about death more like the Amish view. Amish relatives mourned but it seemed easier for them to be certain the Lord has a plan, and the departed was in a better place.

Jennet and Ian had arranged for a small family funeral service for Nettie. That, too, was a good thing as far as Hannah was concerned. It would only hurt Jennet if she planned a big service and nobody came. Hannah doubted if Jen knew how few friends Nettie had left in the community. Her popularity had waned since she'd married Bob. Even with Jen. At one time Jennet was a routine visitor to Chelsea Township. Her visits had become more and more infrequent about the time Nettie remarried. Of course, Jennet's traveling career accelerated around the same time and it might have been only coincidence. Maybe. Lots of coincidences. Some more things to gently explore with Jen.

Looking at Jennet now sitting in a leaf printed wing chair in Caroline's family room, Hannah thought Jen looked like a fragile, wilted flower caught in a jungle thicket. Her eyes, enormous in a pale, peaked face, looked bruised by dark shadows. Ian sat close by on the footstool watching her, his gaze solicitous and loving. Just the way Stephen looks at Carrie, and neither Jen nor Carrie can see it, Hannah observed.

Carrie was treating Stephen more kindly as time went on. She might just be coming around; Hannah would have to keep a good thought. Carrie had invited him to stay for dinner, and he was in the kitchen helping her prepare the meal. Hannah, setting the table, watched them. Now, that was a sight you wouldn't see in an Amish kitchen - a man working side by side with a woman, fixing a meal. Such cooperation wouldn't hurt an Amish man. After all, the women worked in the fields whenever they had a minute to spare from the mountain of household chores which they faced day in and day out.

"Dinner will be ready in about a half an hour," Caroline said. "Why don't you take Ian and Jen into the living room, Granny? There is a fire laid and ready to start. Stephen and I will be there shortly."

Hannah knew her opportunity to question Jen and Ian when she saw it. She had discussed with Stephen and Carrie the questions she would ask. How to work her way into the questioning was the problem. Tactfulness wasn't natural to Hannah and subterfuge was almost completely alien. She did not want to think Jennet could have had anything to do with the murder of her sister, but personal feelings could not get in the way of a thorough investigation.

"Hannah," said Jennet, breaking the silence once they were seated in the living room, "do you think that police chief, Benton isn't it, knows what he's doing?"

"How do you mean?" Hannah asked, surprised Jen had noticed, but not surprised she had asked Hannah's opinion. Jennet knew of Hannah's interest in solving mysteries.

"Ian and I have been talking it over, and neither of us think this Benton person is very with it. He is automatically assuming this man who left footprints is the one who was responsible for Nettie's ...murder." Jennet spoke softly with a catch in her voice. "Ian and I are journalists, but neither of us is familiar with crime. Just the same, it seems to us the police are going about this rather inefficiently."

"I have had my doubts, Jennet, about Kiel Benton. What little he is doing is being done correctly, but he is not seeing the forest for the trees." Hannah didn't share her theory about Nettie knowing her killer. Jennet and Ian were still suspects until proven otherwise.

"Granny Hanny," Jennet said, with an intensity in her tone, "I know it's a lot to ask you, but would you help investigate this case? You knew Nettie and Bob. You live next door, and Caroline was Nettie's attorney. Who better to help?"

"I cannot guarantee I can solve Nettie's murder, Jen. But I will do my best," Hannah said. "To conduct a proper investigation, I must put any personal feelings aside."

"Of course, Granny. I realize I'm included as a suspect along with everyone else," Jennet answered. "I didn't always get along with my sister."

"Not getting along with someone is one thing, hating them enough to kill them, quite another thing," Hannah said.

"Quite," Ian said, from what had become his accustomed place beside Jennet.

"Jen," Hannah began. "Where were you early yesterday morning?"

"In Manhattan, Hannah. Up until nine o'clock, I was at my apartment. Then I went out to breakfast and on to a photo shoot at Marfus Enoon at eleven."

Hannah had pulled out her notebook and was busy taking notes. At the sound of the unfamiliar name, she looked up quizzically. "Who? Or is it what?"

Jen laughed for the first time since she'd arrived. "It's who! He's the hot new designer this year."

"Oh," Hannah said, unimpressed. "Was anyone with you? At your apartment? At breakfast?" She glanced at Ian, wondering if he lived with Jennet. *Caroline seems to think I know nothing of such things. What an innocent she is,* Hannah thought, *to think I am so unobservant.*

"No, Hannah. I was alone. I live alone," Jen said, pointedly. "Up until eleven o'clock, I can't prove where I was. I guess I'm still a suspect."

"How do you think you could be in Lancaster County at eight and back in New York City at eleven?" Hannah asked.

"I could have hired a plane and flown back," Jen said.

"But you didn't, my dear," Ian said.

"I do not think for a minute she did, Ian," Hannah said. "But I had to ask."

"I was at a meeting in Boston," Ian said. "I arrived there Wednesday and returned to New York on the noon plane yesterday."

66

"Oh, Ian," Jennet said. "Why would Hannah ask your whereabouts. You didn't even know my sister."

"Quite. But, I told her anyway. What if we'd been in cahoots?"

"Thank you, Ian," Hannah said, as seriously as she could manage. The strain must be getting to Ian. She could just see it now. A world famous financial commentator, well known by sight to the public, sneaking into Amish country, dispatching the twin sister of his girlfriend with a butcher knife, then returning to carry on as usual. She had better get this investigation back on track. Now.

"To figure out who did kill Nettie, we need to know all you know, Jen. You said you didn't always get along with her?" Hannah asked, hoping Ian's presence wouldn't inhibit Jennet.

Ian must have had the same thought. "I shall let you two talk privately," he said. "I need to make a few telephone calls, and now seems to be a good time. Unless you need me for anything else?" Hannah wasn't sure if he was asking her or Jen. Hannah shook her head.

Jennet made no move to stop him. So Hannah was right; Jen did prefer to talk to her alone.

"Actually, Nettie and I still spoke on the phone all the time until she died. I tried to forget the past, but it was hard. One can forgive, Hannah, but forgetting isn't quite as easy."

"You two used to be so close," Hannah said, the still vivid picture of the adorable little girls Annette and Jennet used to be blurring her objectivity.

Hannah knew about Doc Hope's will. Nettie had told her Jennet was angry, although Nettie also swore she hadn't put her father up to anything. According to her, he'd changed his will under his own volition. Hannah was trying to encourage Jennet to talk, not put words into her mouth.

"We always were close until around the time she married Bob Adams," Jennet said. "Then things gradually fell apart."

"How do you mean?"

"We used to visit each other three or four times a year."

"Yes, I remember," Hannah said.

"At first, it seemed natural that Nettie and Bob wanted to be alone, so we stopped exchanging visits. But they never started again. Nettie always had some excuse why I shouldn't come visit, or why she couldn't get to New York. Then, as you know, Hannah, a year after they were married, our father died."

Hannah remembered well Doc Hope's long illness from cancer and his subsequent death. The twins had taken turns staying with him the last few weeks. When his will was read, everything went to Nettie with a notation specifying: "Jennet's lucrative career left her well provided for."

"I was shocked and terribly hurt," Jennet said. "I know Nettie influenced Dad to cut me out of the will. Even the phrasing in the document sounded like Nettie's words, not Dad's, nor his lawyer's. It wasn't the money. It was that my own sister could do such a deceitful, cruel thing. Nettie didn't need the money either. She just wanted what I had. She always did."

Jennet's eyes filled with tears. "I loved Nettie, Hannah, despite what she did. But, how it hurt. It still does." Large tears fell unchecked down Jennet's cheeks and splashed onto her blouse.

Hannah fished in her pocket and handed her a plain white handkerchief. "Do you think Bob had anything to do with it? I thought he was well off financially."

"I'm sure he encouraged her. He was out to get everything he could. I guess Nettie found that out when he took all the money and left her. In a way, Hannah, I couldn't help but think she was well rid of him. He drank too much and was a womanizer as well."

"How did you know that?"

"The usual way. He made pass after pass at me, little innuendoes and double entendres. I was very uncomfortable around him."

"It does not surprise me. Not much does," Hannah answered, sadly.

"The man was a lot like Nettie. They were both spoiled all their lives. Got everything they wanted. Bob was an only child, raised by a mother who traveled all over the world, leaving him with indulgent housekeepers. First his mother ignored him, then she'd arrive home and lavish him with attention. I suspect he married Nettie because she was a replacement for his mother, Eva Adams."

Hannah was taking notes as fast as she could and wishing she knew shorthand like the policewoman, Peg McCoy. "Why did Nettie marry him?"

"She never really told me. She had been divorced from Peter for years, then suddenly married Bob. I didn't even know she knew him, other than that he was a kid in the neighborhood when we were growing up. We were in our teens when he was born. I actually babysat for him once when Annie Shoop was sick. She was the Adams' housekeeper then."

"That is right," Hannah said. "I had almost forgotten. Course everybody is connected with everybody else around here."

"Anyway," continued Jennet, "I tried to be somewhere else when Bob was there alone. Nettie was pretty unpleasant to be with as well. When Bob was around, she was an angel. When he wasn't, she was a shrew. Poor Kate took the brunt of it."

"Jen," Hannah said, as gently as she could. "Do you think there was any possibility Kate was being physically abused…in any way?"

Jennet turned even paler. "Physically? What are you trying to say, Hannah?"

"I am not trying to say anything. I am asking. Do not read anything into that, Dear."

"Not that I knew. Believe me, Hannah, if I'd even had an inkling anything like that was going on, I would have done something," Jennet said in an undertone of fury.

"I am sure you would have."

"I didn't like the way Nettie was treating Kate, but I don't think she would have ever physically hurt her, or let Bob do anything."

"If she knew..."

"Hannah, do you have any reason to think Kate was physically or sexually abused by Bob Adams? Has Kate said anything?"

"She hasn't made any accusations, if that is what you mean. All I know is that she says she hated both her mother and Bob and she will not talk about Bob at all."

"Thank God I talked Nettie into sending Kate away to school," Jennet said. "I figured it had to be better for Kate. Poor kid couldn't stand Bob, and Nettie was a monster to her. I don't want to play amateur shrink, but I'd say Nettie was jealous. Even at thirteen, Kate was beautiful."

"She still is. You have not seen her lately, have you?"

"I've wanted to, but she wants nothing to do with me. Maybe things can be different now," Jennet said.

For both their sakes, Hannah wished it could be, but she didn't hold out much hope.

"It may take a while, Jen. That young lady has a lot of growing up to do first, and she is carrying a lot of resentment around."

"And I remind her such a lot of her mother. Right?"

"Afraid so. Kate has not learned to look inside a person," Hannah said. "Nettie told me she and Bob decided to send Kate away because of behavior problems; she was getting too hard to handle. Said it was her idea."

"After I suggested it," Jen said. "I even asked Nettie to let Kate go to school in Connecticut so I could keep an eye on her."

"Instead, they sent her to school in Arizona."

"She was there only one semester before Peter sued for custody. What a mess," Jennet said. "At least Nettie didn't blame me because she lost custody. This may sound awful, Hannah, but I don't really think she cared for Kate at all."

"Why in the name of <u>Himmel</u>... sorry, I mean heavens, would Nettie fight Peter's custody suit then?"

Jennet sighed. "Because Peter wanted his daughter. Nettie had to have whatever anyone else wanted."

"That is sad."

"Sad and sick, Hannah."

Hannah saw Jennet's shoulders visibly slump and a look of deep dispair return to her face. It was time to get her mind off of Kate.

"Jen, I would like to look at Nettie's house tomorrow. Would you like to come?"

Jennet's hand, in the process of brushing her hair from her eyes, stopped in midair, then fluttered like a falling bird. She caught it with her other hand, and clutched them together. "Oh, Hannah, I don't know if I could. Let me think about it."

"Of course, Dear. You do not have to decide now. Do you know who had a key to Nettie's house?"

"No. I know I didn't. I don't think anyone did. After Bob disappeared, she had all the locks changed and the alarm system installed."

"Well, we can arrange with the police to let us in. I will have Carrie call that Benton man."

"Nettie was absolutely paranoid somebody would break in," Jennet said.

"She told me that, too. I suggested she move into town, but she would not have it," Hannah said.

"It was almost as if she was waiting for Bob to come back," Jennet said.

"Or was afraid he would," Hannah added.

CHAPTER FOURTEEN

Hannah was right when she predicted Jennet would not want to visit Nettie's house the next day. But she did want Hannah and Caroline to go there to pick out and deliver clothes for Nettie to be buried in. Ian had volunteered to accompany them, ostensibly to help with anything heavy. Caroline suspected he sensed there might be danger, and, to quote Hannah, "There is safety in numbers already."

The weather had turned nasty, and a surly looking, lead-colored sky promised rain before the day's end. As Caroline and Ian turned into her father's driveway to pick up Hannah, Caroline's sister, ten-year-old Bethany, was waiting to greet her.

In the past few months, Bethany, who up to then had been petite, had shot up in height. She reminded Caroline of a little colt - all legs. According to Hannah, Bethy looked exactly like Caroline had at her age, with thick hair, the color of corn-silk, and dark blue eyes. Dark brows gave her face an engaging seriousness, but did nothing to spoil her beauty. Today, she was wearing a deep purple dress under her white apron. The reflection made her eyes look as violet and as soft as spring pansies.

71

"I say, what a lovely child!" Ian exclaimed. "Both you and she favor your grandmother. Hannah must have been striking when she was younger. Actually, she still is a beautiful woman."

Caroline didn't comment. She had never gotten used to compliments. One of the main Amish tenets was "Be not proud," and they took it to mean not standing out from their fellows. Conformity was their way, down to dress and hairstyle. Even the Amish who dealt with the outside world every day felt embarrassed at compliments, especially personal ones.

This was an Amish off-Sunday when the family wasn't attending church. Caroline explained to Ian that the Amish held church services every two weeks at various members' homes which could mean up to an hour's buggy ride each way in addition to a three hour church service. On the off-Sunday, no work was done, but visiting and various leisure pursuits and games were permitted.

The Miller family carriages sat, unhitched, in the shed beyond the driveway. The large, gray-topped carriage was used at various times by the family members. An open buggy sat alongside. A bright red sign proclaiming "Milk, naturally!" was next to the triangular slow moving vehicle indicator on the rear bumper.

"That's quite surprising," Ian said, indicating the bumper sticker. "I wouldn't think an Amish carriage would be decorated in such a frivolous fashion."

"It's my brother Josh's buggy," Caroline said. "He's only eighteen and just now joining the church. Before a man settles down, he's allowed to do all kinds of things a church member can't. The elders figure that way he'll get it out of his system. Besides, those signs are popping up all over the place. I think it's overlooked as long as the buggy belongs to a dairy farmer, which, like so many in Lancaster County Amish, my dad is."

Rebecca and Daniel, Caroline's parents, came out on the porch when they saw that Caroline had a passenger. The Amish were as curious about non-Amish as the other way around.

Daniel Miller, a dairy farmer all his life, was a powerfully built man with a massive chest and forearms. His curly, red-gold beard spilled onto his chest like a lion's mane. Today, because it was a Sunday, he was dressed in a plain white shirt and black broad fall trousers. Because the Amish religion eschewed zippers on trousers, the trousers were made with a buttoned flap front and were held up by suspenders.

Caroline introduced her parents to Ian. Rebecca Miller politely offered Ian food, which was something the Amish did on every occasion.

"Thank you just the same," Ian said. "But we just finished one of Caroline's proper English breakfasts with tea, scones, sausage, and eggs. I don't think I could eat another thing until dinner. She's quite a cook."

Rebecca looked disappointed. "Next time you will eat with us?" Caroline's mother was reed slender with brown hair pulled so tightly into a bun that the scalp showed through along the part line. Lines etched the skin around her large blue eyes. She looked drawn, as if she had been without sleep. As the district's most sought after midwife, and in an Amish community where the average number of children was eight, she was busy indeed.

"We'll look forward to it," Ian said.

"How's the baby business, Mom?" Caroline asked.

Busy, like always, Carrie. I was up all night. But Mattie Yost has an eight pound boy. Named this one Benuel. Makes ten for them," Rebecca answered.

"Ten boys?" Ian said, looking amazed.

"That is right. Good thing, too. They have one of the biggest farms in the district," Daniel answered. He explained to Ian that it took many children to work the farms since the Amish didn't use modern farm machinery, but relied on horses.

"Your people are real ecologists," Ian commented.

"We believe we are stewards of the Lord's land. We may use it, but not abuse it."

"That is quite admirable, Sir," Ian said.

"Do not hold much with 'Sir'. Just Daniel will do."

Caroline left them talking and went to find Hannah. She met her coming out of the grossdotti house.

"Sorry. I did not hear your car," Hannah said. "Was putting the final touches on one of my quilt orders. This detective business is not helping me catch up. Course I am usually behind. Too much interesting keeps happening. Think I should take up lap quilting like that lady on TV?"

"Amish lap quilting?" Caroline asked, raising one eyebrow. "Don't think so, Granny. Maybe you should give up the detecting."

"Wish I could," Hannah answered, suddenly serious. "I just hope and pray nobody else turns up murdered."

After extracting Ian from her parent's clutches, although he was a willing prisoner, Caroline, Granny and Ian were on their way to the Adams.

"I hate to leave so soon," Ian said. "Your family is fascinating. I didn't know anything about the Amish. It is really not surprising all those tourists are so interested."

"Yes. Over five million last year," Hannah said, looking dour. "We do not mind them visiting, but they do make it hard sometimes to get on with our lives. Most of them are real nice folks, but there are always a few ..."

Caroline had called Chief Benton and arranged access to the Adams' house. A key was found in Nettie's handbag, and would be turned over to

73

Caroline, as Nettie's attorney. For the time being, there was a 24-hour-a-day police guard posted at the house in case the murderer had been searching for something and might return.

The house stood under lowering skies, looking exactly like the quintessential haunted house. Caroline had a momentary fancy Nettie Adams' ghost was already in residence. Get hold of yourself, girl she cautioned herself silently. Despite the advice, goose bumps rose on her arms.

The house was completely encircled by a garish yellow police ribbon emblazoned, "Crime Scene. Keep Out." A lone police car was parked in front. As Caroline pulled up, a sleepy looking patrolman got out of his car and handed her a key.

"You might want to have things kinda' cleaned up," he said. "I mean before you let the family in. Looks..uh, sorta' messy, you know?" he added, almost apologetically.

"Thanks for your concern, officer. I'll do that," Caroline said. She'd be surprised if Jennet ever wanted to go in Nettie's house, or if she'd need to, after the contents of Nettie's will were revealed.

"The place, or the scene of the crime as they say, looks the same," Hannah said. "Except that Nettie is no longer here." They let themselves in the front door and switched on the bank of lights. "The police did not mess it up more. Sometimes they take big hunks of carpet and wallpaper, that kind of thing, for evidence."

Ian looked visibly shaken. It wasn't too surprising considering there was dried blood everywhere on the steps and the walls. Light filtered in from the landing window making it easy, even from the bottom of the stairs, to see the empty chalk outline of Nettie's body. Even Caroline, who was prepared, and had seen death scenes before, felt queasy. At least that smell of blood had dissipated, being replaced by the overlying odor of chemicals the police used in gathering evidence. The furnace was off, and the house was icy cold.

"Ian," Hannah said, immediately taking charge. "see if you can figure out why it is so danged cold in here. Do you know about American furnaces?"

"A bit, although I must say I know more about boilers. I suppose the furnace is in the basement. I'll give it a go," he answered. Caroline thought he looked relieved to be given a task away from the grim reminders of murder.

"Come on, Carrie," Hannah said, after he had gone. "Let's get upstairs. Watch your step; the stairs might be slippery from some of the stuff the police used to gather forensic evidence. Don't worry about the blood; it is dried." Hannah deftly gathered up her long skirt and cloak, folding them into one hand, and climbed the stairs.

"What are we looking for, Granny?" Caroline asked as she gingerly followed her grandmother upstairs.

"I don't know. Yet. We will start with Nettie's desk. It is in her sitting room right off the bedroom. First, we look for the obvious. Then look for anything hidden, for anything that seems odd to you. Use, as they say in the books, your gut feelings. And, Carrie, we look at everything as if it was real important. Because it just might be. It just might be."

CHAPTER FIFTEEN

"I'd feel like I'm in Hell except it's too cold," Caroline said, shivering from the cold as she looked around at still obvious signs of a struggle which littered the landing and led into the bedroom. Besides obscene blood spatters on walls and pale blue carpeting, a vase lay broken, a small table was overturned, and the scent of crushed chrysanthemums bore witness to the life and death battle which took place on the landing.

"If I know Nettie," Hannah said, peering into the master bedroom, "I mean, knew Nettie, the bedroom is where she would hide anything she did not want found, not in such an obvious place as her sitting room. We'll look there, too, but we start in the bedroom. I'd say that is where the killer found her."

"Or where she brought the killer," Caroline observed.

Hannah glanced at Caroline sharply. "Very good, Dear. You are learning a bit about detecting."

Nettie's bedroom was in a similar state as the hall. Dark red blood splatters contrasted grotesquely with the delicate floral wallpaper and marred the pristine pastel pink and aqua quilt bed covering and white dust ruffle on the brass bed.

"By the looks of it," Hannah said, "Nettie's attacker struck in here first, and the struggle continued out into the hall. Look at how neat the far side of the room is."

Nettie's bedroom looked as if it had been split in half. One side was in complete disarray, and the other looked like a photograph from a decorating magazine. An intricate Amish quilt in a design of roses highlighted one wall. Below it was an upholstered love-seat covered in white brocade. It had been a beautiful room. Plantation shutters were open on each side of an arched bay window, which contained a window seat on which were displayed still more neatly folded Amish quilts. The king-sized, canopy bed, swathed in white tulle, sat against one wall. Hannah knew from previous visits that one door led to a closet and another to a dressing room and bath. The third door led to Nettie's sitting room.

"I am going to follow my theory that Nettie knew her murderer," Hannah said. "So, she must have brought the killer up here for a reason. Why?"

"I can think of several," Caroline said. "Some are not very admirable."

"If you mean sex, say so. Stop acting so prissy, Carrie. We are both adult women. I may be Amish, I may be old; I may not have any first-hand experience with what goes on with the English. But I do know it <u>does</u> go on. A person does not have to speak French to know it when she hears it."

Caroline laughed. "<u>Oui. Touché, Grand mere.</u>"

Hannah's concentration was on her investigation and she ignored Caroline's retort. "Anyhow, I do not think she brought a lover up here."

"Why?"

"One, the bed is made. If she was planning a morning of passion, the bed would be neatened, but tuned down. Two, Nettie was dressed for company, not for lovemaking. She wasn't wearing provocative lingerie, but ordinary stuff under her clothes. I noticed when I discovered the body."

"What if she brought some repairman up here?" Caroline asked.

"Good thought, Carrie. You may have the makings of a fair investigator yet." To herself Hannah thought Annette Adams was too controlled to grab a workman for sex, but as on the other hand, we need to be careful about assumptions.

"I doubt it, Granny. I don't have either your patience nor your enthusiasm for it. I'm just picking up your way of thinking. Say the killer was some kind of workman. Maybe we should look around and see if there's anything obvious that's broken, or if we can find signs of recent repair. Something like the plumbing?"

"It is a starting place," Hannah answered. "It will take a sharp eye to spot something; the house is only a few months old."

The furnace banged on, and a faint odor of heated dust filled the air. "I see Ian knows something about furnaces," Caroline said. "Maybe his talents extend to plumbing. We could ask him to look for some possible repair when he comes back."

"Why don't you go down to the basement and ask him to check around the whole house for something which may have been newly fixed?" Hannah said. "It will keep him busy and out of our way. Poor fellow seems like a fish out of water around the scene of a murder. I swear he looked green as spring peas when he saw the downstairs."

Carrie's theory about a workman was good as far as it went, Hannah thought when she was alone. Problem being: what about the footprints? A repairman would be driving a car, not walking. A fellow intent on murder, especially with a knife, would want to get away quick-like. Nettie was not raped, not that it proved much. The fellow might not have had a chance if she put up a fight. There was only an outside chance, at least in Hannah's way of thinking, that two people could have been involved, the killer, and the man who made the footprints. It was pretty unlikely since Hannah herself had been on the scene so soon after the murder. The killer would have had to get away without leaving any footprints of his own, and, considering the amount of blood, it seemed almost impossible. Then the second man would have had to have somehow stumbled on the murder and fled, leaving his footprints. An almost impossible scenario, let alone a likely one. Nope. There was just one murderer. And Nettie had to have known him.

Was Nettie Adams involved with someone? Maybe, but Nettie knew Hannah was coming over and Nettie would hardly have had her lover around, unless he had spent the night. If he had, there might be some sign. Could be hairs from shaving in the sink, or maybe he left something behind. Hannah knew from Nettie that she packed all Bob's things away.

Hannah began a systematic search. There was nothing in the elegant bathroom to indicate that anyone but Nettie had used it, unless Nettie had thoroughly cleaned it, which was possible.

Hannah opened a cupboard behind the mirrored vanity. Dozens of jars and bottles stared back at her, precisely arranged in alphabetical order. All female fixings. Nettie must have hundreds of dollars worth of beauty preparations in there. Hannah wondered how she used them all.

The rest of the bathroom was immaculate. Mirrors gleamed and the sink and Jacuzzi tub shone, reflecting prisms of light from the crystal fixtures. Healthy green ferns curled and tumbled from porcelain pots on the window sill. The place is clean enough to suit any Amish woman, Hannah thought, not that any Amish woman would have such ostentation. Hannah's own bathroom was about as fancy as an Amish home could boast. It contained a functional, modern bath with a handheld shower massage. Any woman almost seventy needed a few creature comforts, Hannah rationalized when she had it installed.

There wasn't anything hidden in any obvious place. Of course, if Nettie wanted to hide something, there were dozens of places to secrete something permanently. First Hannah would look at the most conspicuous hiding places.

Going into the bedroom, she checked the sheets. Nettie had slept alone on one side of the bed. It was creased, and a faint trace of lipstick Nettie must have missed removing, marred the pillowcase. The other side was as freshly pressed as if it had just come off the ironing board. Hannah was just starting on the rest of the bedroom when Caroline and Ian came in.

"I gave the furnace a go," Ian said, averting his eyes from the bloody side of the room. "Caroline told me about the theory of a workman being on the place. I didn't see anything that looked just repaired downstairs. But I'll have a look round up here."

"Thank you, Ian. The heat feels good," Hannah said. "When you finish up here, maybe check the attic and take a look outside?"

"Righto," Ian answered, going into the bathroom.

"I have not found any signs of another person sleeping here which eliminates the idea of a lover," Hannah said. "At least not one who spent the night before Nettie was killed. I found nothing hidden in the bathroom, nor any signs of anything irregular there."

"You want me to help you search in here?" Caroline asked.

"You bet! There are dozens of places to look. Start with the dressers. Look under drawer linings; feel for papers inside clothing; take out drawers and see if anything is pasted to the bottoms or backs. I'll check the furniture."

The two began a search interrupted only by Ian reporting there were no recent repairs on the second floor. Hannah sent him up to the attic to continue looking.

Hannah removed cushions and unzipped their covers. She searched the bed and looked under it. Then she unfolded and refolded the pile of quilts on the window seat. She unscrewed the brass tops on the bedposts and peered into them with a flashlight. "Nothing. I am about to run out of places to look in here. Course there is the rest of this house. It will take days to search. Still and all, if Nettie was going to hide something, I know it would be in here. She would want to keep it close. Nettie was what they call a control freak. That type keeps important things as close to them as possible."

"Where do you learn this stuff?" Caroline asked. "Never mind answering. I know - the library. How about her purse? That's close."

"Nope. I looked already."

"You looked? When? Don't the police have it?"

"I looked after I found the body. It was right on the table in plain sight. I was seeing if she was robbed," Hannah said. She still felt uncomfortable looking in anyone's purse, no matter what the circumstances. It was such an invasion of privacy. But then so was murder. In a big way.

"And?"

"There was close to a hundred dollars in her wallet. I would have noticed if there was anything unusual in there. Just the usual Nettie stuff. Lots of cosmetics, contact lenses, keys, checkbook."

"What about a safe?" Caroline asked.

"I know Nettie did not have a safe. She told me she was thinking of installing one, but hadn't gotten around to it. She did not even keep one at her shop for money. She said everyone paid by credit card anyway."

Caroline poked her head out of the closet where Nettie had built-in dressers. "Maybe she installed one and didn't tell you."

"Anything is possible. I will look." Hannah had already removed two paintings from the walls to check their backs. "Look along the walls behind the clothes in there. Also, see if the carpet is tight against the floor."

Hannah looked behind the shutters and found only blank wall. Her glance wandered to the remaining wall. The quilt! "Carrie!" Hannah called. "Help me get this quilt down!"

"I looked there, Granny," Caroline said, emerging from the closet. "There isn't anything on it or behind it."

"It is not the quilt I am interested in," Hannah said, excitedly pulling a chair over to where the quilt was hanging. "It's the pole it is hanging on. Nettie had a special pole designed for hanging quilts. You are taller than I am. Climb up and pull the front of the pole from the back. Careful of the quilt."

It took Caroline a few minutes to figure out the pole which Hannah explained was made in three pieces. The back was bolted to the wall and the two front pieces clamped together with the quilt sandwiched between. The front part was a half-round piece of wood, hollow all along its length.

"Nettie had the holders hollowed out so there would be room to roll the top edge of the quilt. That way it could be clamped onto the back without putting holes in it or sewing anything onto it," Hannah said. She and Caroline lowered the quilt and holder onto the love-seat and unscrewed the two parts of its holder.

"Looky here!" Hannah shouted. Inside the front of the holder were four rolled pieces of paper. "Looks like letters. Letters Nettie <u>really</u> did not want anyone to see, or to find."

CHAPTER SIXTEEN

"Good thing I remembered the poles," Hannah said, as she smoothed out the letters, then sat on the floor to read them.

Caroline could see all four sheets were in the same feminine looking penmanship. "Not love letters by the look of the handwriting. Right?" she asked, as she laid the quilt on the bed.

Hannah looked up at her granddaughter. "Anything but. It is blackmail, plain and simple."

"You're kidding!"

"They are pretty straightforward. 'pay up or else' type. Mentions some woman named Betty Burnside. I have never heard of her."

"What does she say?" Caroline asked, trying to read over Hannah's shoulder.

"Here, see for yourself." Hannah handed three of the letters to Caroline.

Caroline read one aloud. "This is dated almost three months ago: 'I know Betty Burnside. What she told me should be kept hushed up. It would be too bad to spoil things by letting the little kitten out of the bag. But if the price is right, it can be disposed of for good. There is proof and lots of it.' It isn't signed."

"That is the first. None of them are signed," Hannah said.

"What is this person talking about?"

"Good question. She did not want to say in the letter. But the name must have meant something to Nettie. Otherwise she would not use it. I am interested in why Nettie would hide these letters? Why not destroy them?"

"Maybe she wanted to use them against this person. Maybe Nettie was planning to turn her in and she needed proof."

"Could be."

The next letter, dated a month later, was just as vague as to what the blackmail was about. It said Nettie's time for deciding was up and told her to be in a phone booth in a large resort hotel in Lancaster. Obviously Nettie hadn't made the contact as the third letter's tone was more hostile and overtly threatening. "'I can go to your daughter or sister. Would you like that? You have one last chance. Don't blow it'," Caroline read. It was dated October 5th. "What did she do?" Caroline asked. Hannah had just finished the final letter.

Hannah handed it to her.

Caroline read it. "'Be at the Seven Sweets parking lot at twelve midnight exactly on Sunday night, October 30th.' Granny, today is October 30th!"

"Hmm, so it is."

"If you are thinking what I am," Caroline said, "forget it. Nettie's murder is the biggest news in Pennsylvania. There is no way this woman wouldn't have heard about it. She would hardly keep an appointment with a dead woman." She handed the letters back to Hannah who was sitting cross-legged on the thick plush carpeting, looking like an Amish Buddha.

"Not a snowball's chance in hell," Hannah said, examining the letters again. "Still… What is to lose already?"

"Sleep," Caroline said, yawning for effect.

"You do not have to go. Stephen offered to help. He will take me."

"Good. Let him go. I'm not thrilled about tearing around the countryside alone with you in the middle of the night. Somewhere out there is the murderer, you know."

"Oh, I know all right."

"Granny," Caroline began, thinking she would use another tact, "why don't we just try to find this woman by looking in the phone book?"

"Oh, I will, but dollar to a donut there won't be a listing. Meantime, I am going to call Stephen."

Hannah and Caroline spent the remainder of the day searching the house for anything else which might shed light on Nettie Adams' murder, but the letters were all they found. Caroline did check the phone book and there wasn't a listing for anyone with the sir name of Burnside. They didn't mention the blackmail letters to Ian.

Ian methodically searched the house and outbuildings. He reported back that he couldn't find anything that looked repaired, inside or out. Of course, as Granny had said, the house was almost brand new. By the time they were ready to leave, the promised rain had materialized. The few leaves left on the trees fell in slippery, wet clumps on the roads as they headed back to Lancaster.

On the way back, they stopped at the funeral home to deliver the clothing Hannah picked out for Nettie Adams to be dressed in for her funeral. Hannah had chosen what she last saw Jennet wear at wedding shower she had given for Susanna, Hannah's granddaughter-to-be. The outfit consisted of a dress and matching scarf of soft silk. The color was as orange as a fall sunset. "Nettie would like something cheerful," Hannah told Carrie.

To herself, Caroline thought of the television show, "Providence", where a deceased, but reappearing character seemed to be destined to wear the same dress thorough out eternity. That orange would be pretty hard to take everlastingly.

"I met this director chap when we made the arrangements," Ian said. "I'll take the clothing in. I'm glad to spare Jennet this task."

When the they returned to Caroline's house, Jennet looked much more cheerful and rested. She had managed to prepare a simple dinner, which Caroline, worn out after a day of digging through a dead woman's house, appreciated. Even eating was an effort. Cooking for company was the least appealing thing she could imagine.

As Granny had thought, Stephen was eager to help by driving Hannah to the meeting with the blackmailer. Despite being tired, Caroline had to admit she was too involved in the case to let Granny and Stephen go without her. And, on the outside chance the blackmailer didn't know Nettie was dead, someone had to play Nettie. No matter how dark it was in the parking lot, neither Stephen nor Granny could pass for Nettie. Caroline, in a wig, might. The matter of where to find a wig was easily solved. Molly was going to be Snow White for Halloween. The costume included a black wig.

"This wouldn't fool anyone in the daylight," Caroline grumbled, peering into the mirror in her powder room. "It's made out of dyed polyester batting. I look more like the wicked witch than Snow White." She spoke in an undertone, so as not to wake Jennet and Ian who were long asleep at the other end of Caroline's house.

"It is also just a <u>scoch</u> too small. You may be nice and slim, but your head is not," Hannah chuckled. "You look like Davy Crockett in a coonskin cap."

"Granny, this is ridiculous," Caroline said, tugging the wig down and tying a scarf on to help keep it there. "At a distance I might pass for Nettie, but never up close. What am I supposed to do if this woman does show up? Whip of my wig and frighten her into talking?"

"Do not get that close…just close enough to get a look at her <u>and</u> her license number, then Stephen will follow her."

They were taking two cars. Caroline, with Hannah hiding would be in one, and Stephen in the other, ready to either aid them or to trail the blackmailer.

"By the way, I checked with information. There is no one by the name of Betty Burnside listed in the 717 area code, or in the 610 area either. That is the Philadelphia area. I could not find a name even close."

"Maybe we should have called Benton on this," Caroline said.

"What would do the <u>Englishers</u> say..yes, that Bozo, do? Nothing! You know it as well as I do." Hannah answered, pursing her mouth as if she'd tasted something unpleasant.

"Okay, I tend to agree with you. Legally, no crime has been committed. The content of the letters isn't specifically threatening. An exact amount isn't mentioned. Besides, with Nettie dead, there's no one to press charges. It doesn't sound like this person is the killer; wouldn't she want her money first?"

"You are assuming Nettie was going to pay. If Nettie maybe threatened to turn her in," Hannah said, "then she would have a motive. But if Nettie was going to do that, why didn't she? No, I do not think this person is the killer either. Nettie sure would not have invited her in for a cozy chat. This blackmailer was waiting to see if Nettie showed up tonight. There would be no reason for her to come to the house first."

"If she shows, we'll know she's not the killer. Right?"

"Maybe. But if she does not come, it does not prove anything. It most likely means she heard Nettie was dead," Hannah said.

"I hate this whole business," Caroline said. "Murder, blackmail, creeping around in the night. How <u>do</u> you get involved in these things?"

Caroline turned to see Hannah wasn't there to answer. She must have seen Stephen's prearranged signal of blinking headlights and gone to the window to signal him back by closing the blinds.

"Come on, Snow White," Hannah said, handing Caroline her coat. "Stephen is here. We are going to see if it is snowing in hell tonight."

CHAPTER SEVENTEEN

Caroline and Hannah drove together in Caroline's small gray car with Stephen following at a discreet distance in his dark blue Mercedes.

"If I had time to plan this caper right," Hannah said from the back seat, "we would have taken Nettie's van. Maybe this blackmailer knows what kind of car Nettie drives. It is the little things that can trip up the best investigator."

"If I remember correctly from law school, Granny, the word 'caper' means an illegal escapade. It's the blackmailer who's doing something illegal, not us."

"You sound just like an attorney, Carrie. In my detective books 'caper' can be used other ways." Hannah's banter with Caroline was helping take the edge off her nerves. On the outside chance that the blackmailer showed up, this could be a dangerous business. From her books and from her own experience, she knew dealing with anyone outside the law was tricky, especially if they thought you were on the other side. This person might be deranged, armed, or accompanied by others. She was half wishing the blackmailer <u>wouldn't</u> show up.

They arrived a few minutes before midnight at the restaurant, named "Seven Sweets and Seven Sours" for the Pennsylvania Dutch meals it served. All the locals called it "Sevens". There were a few low-voltage lights around the doorways, but the lights in its enormous parking lot were off. During the day, the lot was filled with tour busses and cars from every state of the union. Now it was a dark and deserted expanse of wet concrete. Stephen parked his car across the street at the rear of a closed gas station. From his vantage point, he could see, but not be seen.

Hannah huddled on the floor, a blanket over her. "Let me know right away if somebody comes," she said. "We wait half an hour, no more. It is cold in here already."

At twenty-five minutes after twelve, Hannah was still in the same position. "I think this woman must know Nettie is dead, Carrie. You are right; Nettie's murder is the biggest story in ages. Everyone must know by now." Hannah was disappointed but not surprised that the blackmailer most likely was not going to keep her appointment. If she was not going to come to them, they would just have to go to her. All they had to do was find out where she was. "I might as well sit up. My feet are numb," she said, starting to get up.

"Granny, wait! There's a car coming! Get back down," Caroline whispered. She turned the ignition key and started the car.

"Be careful, Carrie," Hannah said, as she dove down hugging the floor and pulling the blanket over her. She could hear the car draw up alongside. It sounded like it had a big powerful engine. She heard Caroline's electric window go down and rain splash onto the back of the seat.

"I don't know who you are," a woman's voice hissed, "but I know Annette Adams is dead, and you ain't her sister. If you was sent by her, I'll make her the same deal I was goin' to make Annette. Fifty thou' in small bills, and I won't tell about the kid. One of them scandal sheets would pay big bucks. It don't matter to me. Their dough's as good as Jennet Hope's."

"How do we contact you?" Caroline asked, sounding completely calm.

"Oh, I'll be around," the woman answered. The next thing Hannah heard was an engine being gunned, and gravel flying.

She jumped up and looked across the street. Stephen was already on his way after the car.

"What did she look like?" Hannah asked.

"Coarse looking. Maybe 40, and very overweight. Brown hair in one of those frizzy styles. She reeked of fried foods and cigarettes."

"Glad I had a blanket over my nose. How about the car?"

"I'm no expert on cars, Granny. It was big, green maybe. Between the rain and the dark, I couldn't be sure. I'd say ten years old at least and a Pontiac or an Oldsmobile. Stephen will know."

"I hope he at least gets the license number. Maybe if he can stay with her, he will have more than that; maybe he will find out where she lives."

"What do you suppose she meant about the 'kid'?" Caroline asked.

"I do not know, but I would bet Jennet does. She said to tell Jennet and that is exactly what I am going to do."

Hannah and Caroline had been back at Caroline's house over an hour before they heard a soft knock at the door. "Stephen!" they said in unison. They went to the door together. Stephen stood dripping water in a pool on the doormat. He looked like the proverbial drowned rat.

"Don't you own an umbrella, Stephen Brown?" Hannah asked as Caroline took his coat to her laundry room.

"I had to follow this criminal of yours, Hannah, through a trailer park on foot. I thought I'd be a bit less conspicuous without an umbrella. Especially since the only one I had in the car was a red Minnie Mouse thing Molly left in the car."

Hannah shrugged her shoulders. "Even though you volunteered to help on this case, Stephen, I guess this qualifies you for hazardous duty pay."

"Just thanks and a cup of coffee will do."

Caroline returned with several towels and handed them to him.

"Now, you tell us what happened," Hannah said. "You talk while we fix the coffee," she added.

Several minutes later, Stephen was holding a cup of steaming coffee and unfolding his story to the rapt audience of Hannah and Caroline. "I took off after her as you saw. It wasn't easy keeping up. I was afraid to use my headlights. The damn woman drove like a maniac. It was raining so hard by then that I don't think she saw me. At least she didn't act like someone who was trying get away from someone who was following."

"The expression is 'shake a tail', Stephen," Hannah interrupted.

"Whatever." Stephen took a big gulp of his coffee. "Anyhow, she drove about fifteen minutes down Route 734, then cut off down a lane, ending up at a trailer park called Cottingham's Cozy View. It was a broken down old dump overlooking a junkyard. I was too busy following our friend to get a real good view. Anyhow, she's in the furthest trailer back. The thing looks like 1950's vintage. Name out front is A. Wallace. I also got the license number. It is a dark green, 1978 Pontiac Bonneville sedan." He fished a damp piece of paper from his pants pocket and handed it to Hannah.

"You are a top notch investigator, Stephen Brown."

"Thanks, Hannah. But what now?"

Hannah couldn't help but notice the enthusiastic note in Stephen's question."Tomorrow we go see this A. Wallace, assuming she is the A. Wallace on the mailbox. I think you should come along, if you do not mind."

"No, not at all."

"First, I have a few questions to ask Jennet. We still do not know who this Betty Burnside, mentioned in the blackmail letters, is, or how she is connected to this Wallace person. And why she should be blackmailing Nettie or Jennet?"

CHAPTER EIGHTEEN

First thing the next morning, Caroline telephoned her boss, Bryce Jordan, and asked for the week off. She told him she was helping Hannah investigate at Jennet Hope's request.

"Since you are Annette Adams' attorney, Caroline," Bryce said. "I don't really consider this time off. You're handling the estate."

"I'm planning to read the will as soon as the services are over."

"Good idea to get it over with. I don't imagine it's going to sit real well with Mrs. Adams' family," Bryce said.

"I don't know. We'll have to see," Caroline answered.

After she hung up, she thought about the will. Privately she thought Bryce was right. If nothing else, they'd all be unpleasantly surprised. Nettie was full of surprises. Even Hannah commented that she was finding out she hadn't known Nettie Adams as well as she had once thought. Maybe Nettie's family didn't care. Jennet hardly needed the money, and Kaitlin seemed too numbed to be concerned. Caroline wondered how stable Kaitlin Drew was. In Caroline's opinion, there was something really weird about the girl. A gut feeling maybe, but nevertheless... One thing Caroline had learned from

Hannah was to listen to her intuition. Kaitlin's attitude was more than a teenaged dislike for her mother. Caroline would like to see what this boyfriend of hers, Chris something or other, was like. All she knew was that according to Peter Drew, Chris was a parolee and a former drug user. Maybe he'd had the inclination to do away with the mother Kate detested. Perhaps he thought Kate was in line to inherit. What better reason for murder? Did Nettie know Kate's boyfriend? Would she have let him in her house? Not likely.

How did A. Wallace fit into Nettie's, and possibly Jennet's, life? What 'kid' was she referring to in her obscure letters? The idea of confronting that unpleasant woman seemed thoroughly unappealing yet irresistible. Caroline was caught up in this case as much as Hannah was, and Stephen was quickly becoming just as fascinated. Like it or not, he was becoming an ever increasing part of her life.

The old Stephen she knew, loved, and was hurt by so many years ago, seemed like a different person than this present-day man. The old Stephen was irresponsible and selfish; the new one was anything but. Their daughter adored him, and Granny was his biggest fan. Stephen walked out on Caroline when she was pregnant because he didn't want a child. She couldn't forgive that quickly, but seeing him again and getting to know him now made it easier, and forgiveness was coming. She had to admit she was becoming very fond of this new and improved version of Stephen Brown.

It was barely seven o'clock, and Stephen was on his way to pick up Granny. Jen and Ian were still asleep. Caroline left them a note telling them that she and Granny were out investigating the case. The funeral was scheduled for two o'clock with the reading of the will to take place at Caroline's office afterwards. Her secretary, Cathie, had notified the family.

Half an hour later, Caroline, Granny, and Stephen were in his car on their way to confront A. Wallace.

Last night's storm had passed, and it was another glorious, crisp fall day. The sky was marine blue and cloudless.

"Thank heavens you have a housekeeper who can get Molly to school," Caroline said, "and take her trick or treating tonight with her friends. I put her costume in the back seat. I miss her; I'll be glad when this mess is over with and things can get back to normal."

"When are Jen and Ian going back?" Stephen asked.

"Ian's leaving Thursday. He told me last night he has to drive down to Washington for some hearings he's covering. Jen's staying until Friday," Caroline said.

She was beginning to be concerned about Jennet's possible reaction to Nettie's will. It certainly was a surprise to Caroline when Nettie had arrived in her office last month to make the new will.

Caroline's firm, Hepler and Jordan, hadn't previously represented anyone in Nettie's family. Hepler and Jordan was a highly regarded, but small, law firm. Caroline considered herself lucky to be taken on by Bryce Jordan, who was a friend of one of the partners, Garrett Clarke, in the New York firm she had previously worked for. Despite the death of Robert Hepler five years earlier, his name was still used out of respect to the Hepler family. Bryce planned to continue it until there was no one around who still remembered the firm's founder. Bryce was a man who never forgot a friend. Caroline continued to be impressed by Bryce's integrity and knowledge of the law. His familiarity and respect for the Amish community made him a strong advocate for them.

It was a natural fit for Caroline to be a part of his firm since one of her main reasons for returning to Lancaster County was to help the Amish maintain their way of life. Too many forces threatened them. English laws, developers, and regulations were unfamiliar to them. They needed strong supporters in the English world to help them bridge the two worlds. Caroline may have left the Amish, but she understood and championed their right to maintain their lifestyle.

Nettie decided to go with the firm because Caroline had joined them. As she told Caroline, she wanted a fresh start and she wanted an attorney she knew. Other than to write her will, Caroline hadn't been much use to Nettie. She'd make up for it now, not that Nettie would be around to know the difference.

Granny was uncharacteristically quiet in the back seat as the car purred along. Caroline thought Hannah looked tired this morning. She had been shorted on her usual four hours of sleep. None of them had gotten to bed before two o'clock.

"What have Mom and Daat been saying about your gallivanting about at all hours?" Caroline asked.

"Not much. I do not think they even pay my doings any mind anymore. They are getting used to it. Besides, what they do not know cannot hurt me," Hannah chuckled. "How far is this place, Stephen?"

"Not far, Hannah. About a mile up the road. Hang on when I turn; the road's a mess."

"You ought to try it in an Amish carriage," Hannah said. "Your bones get jarred around. There are worse places to be riding than in a Mercedes already. Well you know. You have an Amish carriage."

"I did. Don't any more," Stephen answered, turning onto a graveled road full of ruts.

"You sold it? Why?" Hannah asked.

As usual it hadn't occurred to Granny it was considered prying to ask the English such personal questions, Caroline thought.

"Not exactly sold," Stephen answered. "Just got rid of it. Decided it was impractical to keep it around when it wouldn't be used except for decoration," Stephen answered.

Caroline, sitting next to him, detected a flush creeping up his neck. "Granny, is your seat belt fastened?" Caroline asked, trying to change the subject. She saw Stephen was embarrassed even if Hannah hadn't caught on.

But Hannah wouldn't be distracted. "Of course, Carrie. Stephen Brown, you mean you gave it away?"

"I sort of traded it," Stephen mumbled.

"Who to?" Hannah asked.

"Joseph Yoder, down the road from me."

"Patches Yoder?" The Amish were fond of nicknames. It was also a useful way to differentiate between so many persons with the same or similar names. Caroline had no idea how Patches Yoder's nickname originated.

"I think that's what they call him," Stephen said.

Caroline knew that Joseph Yoder's carriage had been destroyed by a car a few weeks previously. His oldest son and his wife were seriously injured and were still in the hospital. As is the case with most of the Amish, they probably had no insurance. Joseph was not a prosperous man, but he owned a small apple orchard and had eight or nine young children to care for. He undoubtedly would be financially strapped with medical bills.

"What did you trade it for?"

"Apples," Stephen said. "I'll never run out of apples now."

"Good thinking," Hannah said.

Caroline turned, knowing what she'd see when she looked at her grandmother. She was right; Hannah was smiling.

They turned into a seedy looking trailer park. "God," muttered Stephen. "This place is a worse dump than it looked like last night."

All of the dozen or so trailers were old. Caroline didn't know a thing about them except they weren't the kind she'd seen for years. Most of them looked barely habitable. A leafless tree reached out with gnarled limbs that looked like pleading arms. Two rusty chains, no longer anchored by a swing, swayed from another, smaller tree. Several attempts at a garden were now withered by frost and stood blackened, adding to the forlorn aura of the place. Two broken down cars stood on blocks. A couple of trucks looked about the same age as the trailers. Litter lay everywhere.

Caroline could see the dark green car from the restaurant parking lot standing at the end of the row in front of the last trailer.

"She's there," Stephen said.

"You keep an eye on the trailer, Stephen, in case A. Wallace has a mind to scoot. Carrie and I will pay a visit to the office," Hannah said.

Nailed to a tree in front of the first, and least disreputable looking, trailer was a hand lettered sign which said, "Cottingham's Cozy Acres. By the week or permanent. No peddling. Office."

"Ever felt more conspicuous?" Caroline asked. "Maybe we should have brought my car."

"Still too conspicuous," Hannah said, following her out of the car. "Look at the three of us; we would stand out in any vehicle. Let me talk, Carrie. Just follow my lead."

"It's all yours, Granny."

Hannah rapped on the frame of the screen door several times before it opened.

"Yeah?" A wizened fellow about seventy five, a stubble of gray beard on his chin, opened the door and peered out. "Whadda' ya want?"

"Good morning, Sir," Hannah said cheerfully. "My granddaughter and I need to talk to you."

The fellow in the doorway looked at them doubtfully. "Yeah? What about?" He was dressed in a faded blue aloha shirt and pajama bottoms.

"Wohl, we chust have been looking for my granddaughter's husband's older sister yet." Hannah who normally spoke English as well as anyone, now talked in a thick Pennsylvania Dutch accent. "Her mother-in-law's aunt died and left some money yet. But our kin, the one we have been trying to find, is chust not a well girl. She is ferdutzed... had some mental problems already some time back. We chust did not want to spring this on her unless she is all right yet."

The man looked mystified. "What you want from me?"

"We think," Hannah continued. "She is the same A. Wallace as chust is living in the last trailer there," Hannah waved at the driveway.

"Aggie Wallace? No way is she your relation. She ain't no Dutchy."

"Yah, she is not Amish already. She is my granddaughter's husband's.."

"Skip that rigmarole. I get th' drift. You ain't lookin' for no Dutchy. You lookin' for Aggie. Aggie's kinda strange, all right." The man nodded, then cackled like a strangling chicken, his bony chest rising and falling under his shirt. Even from where Caroline was standing, she could smell the odor of liquor. "And she could use the dough. Don't work if she don't hafta. Owes me rent. So's everybody. So what's new?"

"Yust how long has Aggie been living here already?" Hannah asked.

"Dunno exactly. Can't remember like I used to. Around three years. Since her old man took a hike."

"Oh?" Hannah said, sounding as innocent as a child. "Aggie was married already?"

The man cackled again. "Didn't mean husband, lady. You better ask her. Ain't likely she's up yet. Too early for Aggie. It's the last mobile home in the back." Without another word he closed the door.

"Some mobile homes," Hannah said. "Not mobile, and home is stretching it a bit." They walked back to the car where Stephen was waiting.

Caroline wrinkled her nose. "He was a real charmer," she said under her breath. "I'm only surprised he didn't want money for his 'information'."

"I think he was too confused by me." Hannah said.

"I can see why. Very clever, Gran. You do good work."

"What now, Granny?" Stephen asked after they were in the car and had told him what happened. "Do we all visit Aggie?"

"Darned right," Hannah answered. "I doubt if she is dangerous. The woman wants money. I just do not want her to leave before I am through with her. It would be harder for her to leave with you in the way."

"I'll make it even harder," Stephen said. "I'm going to park Ms. A. Wallace in with my car. She won't get away by car unless she wipes out a couple of trailers."

He pulled his car across the end of the drive, blocking the Oldsmobile, and they got out of the car. Aggie Wallace's trailer was quiet. Yellowed Venetian blinds shuttered its minuscule windows. A rickety looking platform topping three steps had been constructed near one end, leading to a door. With Caroline and Stephen standing behind her, Hannah knocked.

The door flew open so suddenly that Hannah barely had time to step back. Aggie Wallace stood in the doorway. Gleaming in her hand was a large pistol pointed straight at Hannah.

CHAPTER NINETEEN

Hannah didn't move. Not that I could if I wanted to, she thought.

Dressed in shapeless gray sweats, Aggie Wallace blinked against the light. "Oh!" she exclaimed, pointing the revolver towards the decking. "I thought you was... never mind. Sorry about the gun. A woman alone gotta be careful, you know. Who are you?" she asked, apparently just then noticing Caroline and Stephen who had moved in closer to Hannah.

"We are here just to talk to you, Aggie Wallace," Hannah said, as soothingly as she could manage, "about Annette Adams."

"Who are you?" Aggie repeated. She looked frightened and backed against the door. Don't know why she should look so scared, Hannah thought. She is the one with a gun.

"I am Hannah Miller, Mrs. Adams' next door neighbor. This is my granddaughter, Carrie, and her friend, Stephen Brown. Is there somewhere we could talk privately?"

Aggie looked them over. "Okay, but let's make it snappy. I got to go someplace." She stepped aside and motioned them inside, apparently deciding they were harmless, or remembering she was the one who was armed.

Hannah was amazed at the inside of Aggie's trailer. It was as tiny as a ship's cabin, and as tidy. Other than the stink of stale cigarette smoke, the place was immaculate. Two built-in couches lined either side. A galley kitchen with a small built-in table and two benches filled one corner. At the far end, a curtain partitioned another area. I guess I was expecting a blackmailer to be messy, Hannah thought. Or maybe it was because Aggie herself was so unkempt looking.

The place was so small Stephen's head barely cleared the ceiling. "Well, sit down," Aggie said, motioning to one of the couches. Hannah studied Aggie. She was somewhere in her thirties, Hannah guessed. And as overstuffed as a down pillow. Aggie must have once been pretty, but now her face showed the effects of bad habits and plenty of disappointments. Her blond hair was faded around her face and brassy and split at the ends. The corners of her mouth turned down, and deep lines etched her lips from too much smoking and not enough smiling.

"Okay, it's your party," Aggie said to Hannah. "What do you want from me?"

"It is what you wanted from Annette Adams that we have come here to talk about," Hannah said. "We were her friends. We do not want to see her sister or her daughter hurt."

Aggie still stood. And she still held the gun tightly. Hannah couldn't take her eyes off it.

"This is business. I got something to sell; I'm looking for somebody to buy it. Nobody needs to get hurt. That's why I never went to the papers first. We can still keep it quiet." Aggie was gesturing with the gun.

"Will you please put the gun down? You are making me nervous." Hannah said.

"No," Aggie said curtly. "So, you interested in buying information, or not?"

"We do not know what information you are selling," Hannah said.

"It's about the kid."

"Kid?" Hannah said. "What kid?"

"The kid Annette Adams raised," Aggie replied with exasperation. "Kathleen's her name."

Hannah and Caroline exchanged glances. Did Aggie mean Kaitlin. She must, was the unspoken thought Hannah had.

"Yes? Continue," Hannah told her.

"Well, you see this kid ain't Annette's, nor not that dentist's she was married to then either," Aggie said, sounding smug.

97

"And exactly what proof do you have of this allegation?" Stephen interjected, sounding like a lawyer.

"Plenty," Aggie answered. If she was at all intimidated, she didn't sound like it, Hannah thought. Of course she was holding all the cards, not to mention that big gun. Aggie was playing her moment in the spotlight for all it was worth. She was also dragging this out and Hannah was feeling frustrated, but Aggie wasn't going to know it if Hannah could help it.

From the edge in Stephen's voice, he obviously shared Hannah's irritation. It wouldn't do to let Aggie know she was getting to them. Hannah shot Stephen a cautionary look. He nodded his head ever so slightly, indicating he read the warning.

"You have an appointment," Hannah said, standing up, and looking at Aggie. "So do we. Let us stop fooling around and get this over with. You show us your proof. Tell us your terms, and we will decide if you have something to sell and if we want to buy it."

Aggie immediately looked less confident. "Just hang on, and I'll tell you. My ma was Betty Burnside. She's dead now, but she was a midwife up in Centre County. She delivered the kid. And Annette wasn't the mother of it."

Hannah looked incredulous. "That is a ridiculous story."

"It weren't Annette who had a kid; it was the other one who was the mother. It was the sister. You know, Jennet Hope, the big TV star," Aggie said, waving the gun with a dramatic flourish.

"What proof do you have?" Hannah asked, trying to sound composed, but feeling anything but.

"My ma said so, and I was there, too. I remember the women...twins they were. It was real unusual to have some fancy city women at Ma's, except to get rid of kids. My ma used to help in that department, I mean, somebody had to. It weren't legal like it is now," Aggie said. She put the gun on the kitchen drain board and lit a cigarette. "Anyhow, I was a teenager. I remember it real well. It was a real bad labor. Took all day and most of that night. Ma got scared the mother oughta go to the hospital but the sisters wouldn't go."

"This story could easily be invented," Hannah said. "If you are telling the truth, why didn't Mrs. Adams pay for your information?"

"Beats me. Maybe she didn't care if the story got out," Aggie said. "Maybe I were trying to sell to the wrong sister. After all, the one who has the most to lose if this hits the papers is Jennet." Aggie took another drag on her cigarette. The tiny trailer was getting saturated with smoke.

"What real proof do you have?"

"I can tell you what the kid's mother said to the other one. She said: 'It is a good thing you are not going through labor, Nettie. You couldn't stand the pain.'"

Hannah knew the woman was probably telling her the truth. There was no other way she could know about Nettie's aversion to pain. She also refereed to Annette as Nettie. Still, it wasn't hard evidence. "Means nothing," Hannah scoffed. "Show me proof."

"Why would anyone pay you to keep quiet?" Caroline asked. "Even if this story is true, this the twenty-first century.. An illegitimate child isn't a scandal anymore."

"It's still a big deal if you're a famous TV star and your kid thinks someone else is its ma. Those gossip papers love this kinda stuff; they pay big for a story like this."

"Why are you just coming forward now with this story?" Hannah asked. "You've known about it for all these years."

"I ain't much for watching that fashion stuff. I just saw Jennet Hope on TV for the first time. I'd heard she was from around here and I was curious. Recognized her right away; she looked just the same. So I started asking around. I found the sister, Annette owned that quilt store, and went there." Aggie lit another cigarette from the one she was just finishing. "She talked to me real friendly. Said something about her daughter who's almost seventeen. I knew right then, Annette's not the real mother."

"How? Annette and Jennet are identical twins," Caroline said.

"Just keep your shirt on," Aggie sneered. "I'm getting to it. So I come back a couple of days later. I'd gone to a place that sells Zodiac sign charms. See, I remembered the date the kid was born. It was the day before Christmas. So I buy this Capricorn charm, see, and I wear it. Course Annette sees it and asks me the day I was born. I say the day before Christmas, and she goes, 'Oh, what a coincidence. My daughter, Kate, was born that day!'" Aggie looked proud of her ploy.

She is more clever that I would have given her credit for, Hannah thought, blinking. The smoke was starting to make her eyes water.

"You still haven't told us why you thought in the beginning that Annette wasn't the child's mother," Stephen said.

"The one who had the baby had pierced ears. Annette didn't. I could see real plain like on TV that Jennet does!" Aggie said. "You tell Jennet I could get fifty grand from the National Newswatch. For thirty, I'll sell her the same thing," Aggie said.

"I don't think you have anything to sell, Aggie," Stephen said, standing and looming over the chunky woman. "In case you don't know it, the scandal sheets have been the subject of a lot of libel litigation lately. In other words, people have been suing them. They've been hit badly with judgments against them. They won't buy your story without proof. You have only some hearsay and some farfetched ear piercing story. That's not proof. You don't have a damn thing to sell," Stephen said.

Aggie looked deflated for a second before her confidence returned. "Maybe. Maybe not. But I know it's true. And just the same, I don't think 'Miss Famous TV Star' would want her public or her daughter to get hold of this. Give her my message. She has till a week from today to come up with the cash. And cash is what I want. Tell her to bring it here. Or send it with someone. I don't care. Else ways, I go to the kid and the papers." She picked up the gun. "Now get out. I got things to do," Aggie snarled, blowing smoke directly at Hannah.

After they were back in the car, Hannah spoke first. "To quote Aggie, 'I got things to do', too. Namely, to ask Jennet Hope a few questions," Hannah said, looking grim.

CHAPTER TWENTY

"All I can say," Stephen said once they were away from Cottingham's terrible trailer park, "is that's one flimsy story to base blackmail on."

"Maybe so, Stephen Brown," Hannah said. "But I have no doubt it is true. There is no way anyone would know about Nettie's aversion to pain otherwise. Nettie's ears were not pierced. She used to joke that she was the only non-Amish woman who still had intact earlobes."

Caroline sat quietly in the front seat, thinking. How about a birth certificate? If the twins had lied, it wouldn't prove anything. What was their explanation for having a midwife in a distant county delivering the baby?

"Granny, did you know Kate was delivered by this midwife?"

"Sure I knew. But I do not believe I ever heard her name."

"Wasn't that a little odd for someone like Nettie?"

"Not under the circumstances. It was not planned that way. Peter was in the Navy when Nettie was expecting. He had wanted a baby for a long time, but Nettie was not so enthusiastic, and kept putting him off. They had been married for years before Nettie got pregnant. They were living near Frederick, Maryland then. Doc Hope wanted her to come home while Peter

101

was away, but Nettie wouldn't, because she was partners in a co-op antique store in Frederick. Jennet came from New York to stay with her so she would not be living alone." Hannah sat as far forward as her seat belt would let her and peered between the seats so she could look at Caroline. "The way I heard it, the baby was due round Valentine's Day. Anyhow, just before Christmas Nettie and Jen, had gone up the country on a quilt buying trip. Nettie went into labor and the closest help was a midwife. Now that I think of it, I thought at the time it was a funny time to go on a business trip, so close to Christmas yet."

"It all fits," Caroline said. "Jennet wasn't married, but pregnant. Annette was married, but not pregnant, nor did she want to be. Peter was in the service…how convenient. The sisters traded places."

"They were good at that," Hannah said, nodding her head. "They used to do it all the time. Fooled just about everybody, even Doc Hope. Never could fool me, though. Nettie was too <u>debilish</u>. That means devilish, Stephen. It is not polite to speak Dutch in front of <u>Englishers</u>. Sometimes I forget."

Stephen smiled. "Don't worry about it, Granny."

"But I do. There is no excuse for being unmannerly. Anyway, as I was saying, they could not put anything over on me when they were little. I suppose as adults they might have been able to fool anyone, if they wanted to."

"Did you see Kaitlin when she was a newborn? Was she small enough to be, what was it, six or seven weeks premature?" Caroline asked.

"I did not see the baby until late in the spring. She was small, but that does not mean anything. Doc Hope must not have noticed, or at least he never said anything to me," Hannah went on. "I suppose they had to say she was early to make sure Peter could have been the father."

"Do you suppose Peter knew?" Stephen asked.

"I doubt it. He is a very upright fellow. He would never have gone along with the pretense," Hannah said.

"Then who was the father?" Stephen asked.

"Seems to me the one to answer that is Jennet," Hannah said. "Stephen, would you make a little detour on the way to Carrie's?"

"Sure. Where do you want to go?"

"Osgood's Funeral Home. I want to visit Nettie."

"Whatever you'd like," Stephen said, blandly. Peripherally Caroline saw his eyebrows raise quizzically. But she knew exactly why her grandmother had a sudden desire to pay Nettie's body a visit. She wondered the same thing.

They parked in front of the funeral home, which was the most elegant building in the small hamlet of Farmer's Corners, the same town where Stephen's hardware store was located. The red brick building boasted a grand looking striped awing which led from the curb to the imposing double front doors.

The three of them went in through the door which had a sign saying "Enter". The place typified the over furnished, overheated atmosphere of every funeral home Caroline had ever been in. A cloying scent of lilies and chrysanthemums was particularly oppressive in the close air. Their perfumes fought, smelling more like air freshener in a service station rest room than fresh flowers. Long hallways extended in both directions on either side of the entry. A staircase leading upwards was roped off with a sign, "Private."

Granny seemed unsure of which way to go, and Caroline and Stephen, who were behind her weren't much help. Caroline didn't want to call out, so she listened for some clue. At first, she heard only the sound of doleful, recorded organ music. Then she became aware of muffled voices. "This way, Granny," she said, pointing. They followed the noise down one of the somber hallways. A dozen paneled doors shielded rooms whose contents Caroline preferred not to investigate. Yards of plush carpeting muted their footsteps.

At the end of the hallway, a door was ajar and they could hear two male voices. "We only need a few chairs, Frank," one of them said.

A smoked glass door was lettered in gold script, "The Eternity Parlour". Ugh, Caroline thought as she pushed open the door and called out. "Is the director here?"

A man, looking like the antithesis of a funeral director, waved at them from across the room. "I'm Carl Osgood, the director. This fellow is Franklin, my aide-de-camp so to speak. Need some help?" He boomed in a most unfunereal voice.

"He's a dead ringer, excuse the pun, for Santa Claus, isn't he?" Stephen whispered to Caroline as Hannah went ahead to talk to the man. "All he's lacking is the beard."

Carl Osgood conversed with Hannah while Stephen and Caroline stood in the doorway. Osgood's helper, Franklin, a slight man of about thirty, arranged chairs in a half circle at one side of the coffin. It was partially covered with a blanket of the most beautiful and brightest orange roses Caroline had ever seen. "What a waste of flowers," she commented in an aside to Stephen.

She still had an Amish taste for simple funerals where no flowers were displayed. The Amish loved flowers, and every Amish home had blooming and cutting gardens, but they believed flowers at a funeral were both pretentious and wasteful. Flowers were for the living. "Think of how people in a hospital would enjoy these roses," she said.

"You're right," Stephen murmured.

Osgood walked over to the casket and folded back the top half, then left the room.

"Are you sure you want to see Nettie?" Caroline asked as Hannah returned. Caroline was thinking of the last time Hannah had seen Nettie Adams, when she found the corpse.

"Of course. Carrie, I do believe I am tougher than you give me credit for. This is a case. That takes precedence over any personal feelings I might have."

Caroline felt a little foolish. She was projecting onto Hannah the way Caroline herself would feel if she had discovered the body.

Caroline and Stephen joined Hannah at the coffin. It was eerie to see Nettie lying there. Despite the Hope sisters being identical twins, their personalities were so unalike that Caroline would never have mistaken one for another in life. In death, stripped of her unique living individuality, Nettie was indistinguishable from Jennet. It was as if Jennet could be the one in the coffin.

Standing on tip toe, Hannah studied Nettie Adams' face for a minute, then reached down and lightly touched one of the large pearl earrings. She carefully removed it from the dead woman's ear.

Caroline shuddered even though she guessed what Granny had in mind. Gently, Hannah clipped it back on Nettie's ear. "Stephen, I cannot reach to close the top. Would you, please?" Hannah asked.

Stephen nodded, and quietly closed the lid.

Neither Osgood nor his helper were in sight, so they let themselves out and into the fresh air.

"Well, Hannah?" said Stephen after they were in the car and headed towards Caroline's. "I hope you're not going to tell me that was Jennet Hope in Nettie's coffin."

"No, but the thought had occurred to me already. It was Nettie alright, and her ears are not pierced."

"So where does that leave us?" Caroline asked, more for Stephen's benefit than her own. She knew how Granny's mind worked.

"Aggie is telling the truth. Of that I am sure. It is time Jennet tries a little truth herself. She has a lot of explaining to do. And lots and lots of questions to answer," Hannah said.

Caroline didn't say it aloud, but she couldn't help wondering. How far would Jennet go to keep her secret from getting out?

CHAPTER TWENTY ONE

Hannah was wrestling with whether to talk to Jen before or after Nettie's memorial service. Either way, she wasn't looking forward to it. "I know I said I had to put my personal feelings aside, but I do feel kind of heartless," Hannah told Caroline after Stephen let them out in front of Caroline's house.

"It isn't you who has been lying all these years, Granny. Although you haven't asked my advice, I'd wait to talk to Jen until after the will is read this afternoon. I can't tell you why, but please take my advice, and wait until tonight to question Jen."

"You sure know how to drive an old lady crazy with curiosity already" Hannah said.

"You'll find out soon enough."

"I suppose," Hannah answered, her mind already on exactly what she was going to ask Jennet concerning Aggie's story. She was wondering, too, who would be at the memorial service. The notice in the paper specified private, family services. Would Peter and/or Kaitlin show up? At Jen's request, Caroline and Hannah were included. At least someone besides

Jennet and Ian would be sitting in those red plush chairs lined up around Nettie Adams' coffin.

When the small contingent of Hannah, Caroline, Jen and Ian arrived at Osgood's Funeral Home, with the exception of a shining Cadillac hearse, there were no other cars parked in front. The parking lot alongside was also deserted. Of course, they were a bit early, and maybe Peter and Kaitlin were still coming, Hannah conjectured. She hoped, for Jen's sake, that Kaitlin would come, and at the same time, worried she might and that could make things worse if the girl was as uncaring as she seemed at the mall.

Today, Jennet wore an all black dress and coat, unrelieved by even a touch of color or jewelry. Her face, barely visible behind a brimmed hat with a sheer black veil, was as white as death. She looked plainer than the plainest Mennonite or Amish, Hannah thought. Ian looked like an advertisement for the perfection of English tailoring in a pin striped suit of the darkest gray with a silk tie of lighter gray lying against a snow white shirt. A brisk autumn wind whipped at Jennet's veil and the women's skirts as they left the car and entered the building.

Osgood had turned up the heat, making the scent of flowers even more cloying than it was earlier. He greeted them at the door with a more somber demeanor than he'd exhibited earlier, and led them down the hall to the "Eternity Parlour."

Jennet declined Osgood's arm, but walked alongside him. Ian was close behind with Caroline and Hannah following him.

As Osgood opened with the carved doors with a flourish, Jennet paused. Hannah saw a look she could only describe as absolute revulsion pass over Jennet's face. Was it the sight of her sister's casket which caused such a reaction? Maybe it's only this fancy, fussy, funeral parlor with its gilt and flocked wallpaper, Hannah thought. It sure has the same effect on me.

At one side of the room was a curtained family mourning area, its interior hidden from the rest of the room. It's purpose was to afford privacy for anyone who may be overcome with grief to feel comfortable mingling with the other mourners. A small organ and a pulpit were arranged on a dais behind a raised area, where Nettie's casket sat on a bier. On either side, large floor candelabra with unlit, fat, white candles stood like militant guardians.

Without looking directly at the casket, Jen sat down. After everyone else was seated, Hannah took a discreet look at Caroline's watch. Hannah usually carried a pocket watch, since the Amish didn't wear wrist watches because they were considered too decorative, but she'd forgotten it. It was almost time for the service to begin. Osgood's assistant, Franklin, slid in from behind a screen and quietly closed the double doors. At that cue, the sonorous organ music soared from its unseen speakers. Franklin ceremoniously lit the candles. With that, the electric lights were dimmed by someone behind the scenes.

Suddenly, the candles flickered as the outside door flew open and Sadie and Annie Shoop bustled in like two chickens with ruffled feathers. Jennet turned to glance at them briefly, nodded slightly, and turned back to resume her straight backed position. They would come, Hannah thought, despite my making it clear to them that Jennet wanted family only at the services. Could be they considered themselves such. Maybe I am being uncharitable, Hannah thought, but it is more than likely that Annie and Sadie just did not want to miss anything.

Annie Shoop took the chair next to Caroline and Sadie plopped down heavily in the last of the chairs placed around the bier. Reverently, Sadie bowed her head while Annie silently stared steadily at the rose covered, closed casket, not even bothering to acknowledge Caroline's whispered greeting.

The piped—in organ music came to an end as Osgood lifted the hinged casket lid and secured it. It opened away from the audience. Annie's fingers intertwined around each other and she looked at the coffin with round, dismayed eyes. Hannah didn't understand why. It was usual in this area of the country for funerals to be conducted with an open casket for viewing. Maybe Annie was expecting Nettie to join the gathering, Hannah thought intolerantly. Annie, with her overblown reactions, prickled Hannah despite her prayers for understanding and patience.

Osgood stood at the lectern. An ornate Bible, with a tooled leather cover, lay open in his hands. "Friends," he intoned, "Annette Adams was our friend, our sister..." He was interrupted by the doors to the hall opening once again. A draft from the open doorway made the candle flames flicker violently and cast wavering shadows on the wall beyond the platform where the casket lay. Everyone looked towards the door.

Peter Drew, looking Lincolnesque in a black suit with a narrow string tie, stood with his daughter, Kaitlin. Today Kate looked more appropriately dressed for Hannah's taste in a long dark skirt and jacket. It wasn't until she started to walk that Hannah saw the skirt was unbuttoned clear up to the girl's thighs, displaying a sassy red lining, and just about all of Kate's legs.

Franklin appeared from behind the screen and quickly placed two more chairs behind Jen and Ian, forming a second row. Hannah could see them plainly from where she sat. Kaitlin's face was set in a mask. Defiant would describe the look, Hannah decided. Jen turned and smiled briefly at the pair. Peter leaned forward and patted her shoulder, but Kate neither returned the greeting nor made any other move towards her aunt. Don't suppose she has any idea Jennet might be her mother, Hannah thought. Probably would only make matters worse if she did. Or could they be any worse?

Osgood droned through a service of sorts while the background music ebbed and surged like waves on a beach at low tide.

The only relaxed looking person in the congregation was Ian. He sat back in his chair, holding one of Jennet's hands lightly in his, attentively listening to Osgood. The rest of them, each with his or her own agenda and memories sat tensely forward, despite the comfort of the overstuffed arm chairs. Hannah and Caroline were alert and watchful. Sadie looked mournful, Annie still dismayed, Jen tightly controlled, Peter gaunt and haunted-looking, and Kate irritated. The undercurrent of emotions in the room was palpable, like a living, hostile presence. Then came the part of the service Hannah had been dreading, given the volatility in the room. It was time to view the mortal remains of Annette Adams.

Jen was first. She tightly clutched Ian's hand, and for the first time, some emotion played on her face - panic, verging on hysteria if Hannah was any judge. Jennet stood, took a wavering step, and then halted. Ian, steadying her elbow, leaned down and said something to her. All Hannah could catch was "Quite unnecessary my dear." Jennet shook her head, stood taller, and moved up the two steps to the platform on which the coffin rested. She walked right on by, without a downward look or a pause. She couldn't bear to see her sister. Oh, my, thought Hannah. It would be easier for her if she did look. It would help her say goodbye and put some closure to her sister's death. Soon or later she needed to put all this behind her. Everyone had his own way of dealing with such things, Hannah mused. As she often told herself, the Amish way is not the way of the English. The English do have a way of making everything so complicated sometimes. Jennet and Ian returned to their seats, Jennet's face composed once more.

Sadie and Annie were next in line. Hannah watched as Sadie passed by, looked down briefly, and continued on. Then came Annie. Hannah held her breath, waiting for Annie to begin wailing. She didn't. Instead she looked at Nettie, immediately looked at Jennet, then back at Nettie, her eyes darting like a fast flying bird. What in Himmel is she doing, Hannah wondered. Then Annie smiled at Nettie's body like she was meeting her in the store. "Hullo, Nettie," Annie said cheerfully, and hurried back to where Sadie stood watching, at the end of the platform.

"Good grief," Caroline whispered in a barely audible aside.

"Yäh, something like that," Hannah answered in an undertone, as the Shoop sisters returned to their seats.

Franklin, standing at the end of the row, indicated that Caroline and Hannah were next. They passed by the coffin. In death, Nettie looked much more peaceful than Hannah had ever known her to be in life. She wore the bright dress, a garden party style which Hannah had brought. Hannah chose an outfit she knew Nettie liked but one that wouldn't be of much use to

Jennet in the city. Hannah assumed Jennet would take the rest of Nettie's clothes, and no point in wasting a perfectly good garment, Hannah told Caroline with Amish practicality.

As Hannah and Caroline returned, Franklin moved to the second row, and motioned they should go forward. Kaitlin sat impassively as her father held out his hand. "No!" she said loudly. Peter, looking embarrassed, walked alone past Nettie's casket. Hannah felt his distress keenly. Every nuance of the man, his walk, the set of his shoulders, his craggy face, appeared distraught. He looked every inch the grieving widower, not the hostile ex-husband. Hannah looked at Caroline and saw the same unspoken thought on her face. He still loved her... the poor fellow.

Finally, mercifully, the service was over. Hannah thought it was a shame when the person officiating at a funeral didn't even know the dead person. Osgood had never met Nettie. He probably used the same service for everyone. All he did was substitute the name.

Hannah wasn't looking forward to the remainder of the day much either. There was the will to be disposed of, and Jennet to be questioned. What a muddle, Hannah thought, looking around as Franklin motioned for the congregation to stand.

Something caught her eye. She looked, then looked again. No doubt of it, the curtains in the family mourning area moved, closing slightly. Someone had been hiding in that room, watching all of them.

CHAPTER TWENTY TWO

Caroline was reaching for her coat when Granny poked her, pointing to the curtains blocking off the family mourning room. "Someone is in there," Hannah hissed. "Watching."

Caroline reacted instinctively. Despite what anyone in the room might think of her precipitous behavior, and heedless of any possible danger, she dashed over to the mourning area and pulled the curtains apart. As she did, the rear door to the area closed with a decisive click. "Damn," she muttered, knowing she couldn't get around to the outside before whoever was there left. She tried the door; it was locked from the outside. She ran out into the hall. It was empty. Through one of the long windows, she looked out front. There were only three parked cars and the hearse on the street. No moving cars nor anyone in sight. She ran outside, looking around the main parking lot. It was empty.

When she returned, the funeral was over. Hannah was waiting for her at the door to the street. Jennet had decided to let Osgood's take care of the internment. She didn't want to watch her sister go into the ground. Ian volunteered to represent her as he didn't need to be present at the reading of the will scheduled for later in the day.

"Sorry, Gran, whoever it was escaped. Unless he's hiding in the building, he got away. Maybe it was somebody who worked for Osgood."

"I asked Osgood. Only Franklin was on duty. He was in plain sight. Osgood has no idea who would be crashing a funeral. He swears he has never had an incident like this before."

"It's odd. You don't suppose Aggie...?"

"No, she is only greedy, not curious. Maybe Bob Adams has returned from wherever," Hannah mused. "But if he has, there would be no reason to hide, unless he is worried about being a suspect."

"Remember, Granny, the Shoop sisters saw the intruder. It wasn't Bob."

"Right, but we don't know that the intruder fellow was the murderer either. Let us not be assuming anything like our friend, Acting Chief Benton. But I do not think it was Bob. Hiding at the funeral, not coming out in the open, would make him look suspect. If he killed Nettie, he would want to look as normal as possible."

"The grieving husband," Caroline said.

"Yah, the grieving husband." Hannah said. "I sure would like to know where Bob Adams is right now."

They turned at the sound of voices behind them. Peter was walking with Jennet, the two of them making idle conversation about the weather. Of course, Caroline thought. What could take its place as the perfect small talk topic?

Ian had Kaitlin in tow. His charm seemed to be working its effect on her, too. She looked a bit less sullen than usual.

Sadie and Annie were nowhere in sight. That's strange, Caroline thought. Were they still in the Eternity Parlour?

"I'll be right back," she told Hannah, and returned to the room where Nettie's casket lay.

The doors were open, but Sadie stood at the door, blocking Caroline's entrance. Beyond her, Caroline could see Annie kneeling at the coffin. Although her lips were moving, Caroline couldn't hear what she was saying. Was she talking to the dead woman or praying?

"Annie is paying her final respects," Sadie said. "Let's give her privacy."

"I hadn't realized she was that close to Nettie," Caroline said. Hannah had told her how annoying Nettie found the Shoop sisters' constant snooping, and that if they hadn't been such extraordinarily skilled seamstresses, she wouldn't have them working for her. The way they were carrying on now, you'd think Nettie was a member of their family.

Sadie looked offended. "Well, Carrie, you know Annie practically raised Bob Adams. Nettie being his widow and all made her special to Annie. Annie is just real upset by all this. She is not all that strong, you know."

"Of course, Sadie. Annie should have all the time she needs to grieve."

"At least she is able to say goodbye. Don't know what's the matter with Jennet. Seems to me she's pretending Nettie's still alive."

Hannah had come up behind Caroline. "Now, Sadie Shoop, each of us handles death in her own way. You are judging Jennet. Is that not so?" Hannah asked, sternly. Caroline had heard that note in her grandmother's voice many times. Hannah had little patience with judgmental people.

Sadie reddened, but didn't back down. "It doesn't seem fitting…"

Hannah turned away from her. "Come on, Carrie, Ian is waiting for us. Goodbye, Sadie."

"Hannah, wait," Sadie called after them. "What about the internment? Is there an open house?"

Hannah didn't answer, but kept on walking.

"Granny, shouldn't you answer her? Sadie may never speak to you again."

"You are right already. That would be a shame," Hannah said, smiling broadly.

A little over an hour later, a small group sat in Caroline's office. Hepler and Jordan, the law firm she worked for, was located in a beautifully restored nineteenth century house in the heart of Lancaster, or Lancaster City as some people still called it to differentiate it from Lancaster County. The restoration was designed to resemble the warm and gracious home it had once been, and to avoid the look of an impersonal place of business.

Her private office, despite its requisite wall of law books, looked more like an elegant living room than an office. A long, slender oval table of inlaid woods served as her desk. Behind it, an armoire hid the modern computer and communications paraphernalia necessary to run an efficient business.

She had placed a couch and comfortable chairs around the working fireplace. In the room was a diverse group, including Caroline, her secretary Cathie Smith, Jennet, Peter, and Kaitlin Drew. Also present, at Jennet's request, was Hannah.

Caroline wanted nothing more than to get what was proving to be an onerous chore over with as quickly as possible. She sat in the chair closest to the fireplace and began. "This shouldn't take too long. Annette Adams wrote this will only a month ago. When I refer to the executor, I mean myself. I'll skip some of the legalese and get right to it. My secretary will have a copy for all of you afterwards." Caroline cleared her throat. The abundance of flowers at the funeral home had kicked up her allergies. She was starting to lose her voice.

"Besides her clothing, which Mrs. Adams has willed to her sister, Jennet Hope, she wished the rest of her property, real and personal, including her business, Flying Needles, to be liquidated immediately and the proceeds to be held in trust..." Caroline glanced at Kaitlin, who sat smiling slightly, her look frankly expectant. Boy, is she in for a surprise, Caroline thought as she cleared her throat once again. "Sorry. As I was saying ...to be held in trust for the return of her husband, Robert Adams." There was a collective gasp.

Ignoring it, Caroline continued. "There are no other bequests." Caroline finished and looked up to meet four shocked faces. Only Cathie looked normal.

Jennet, sitting by herself, apart from the others on the couch, stood up in one smooth motion. Her face was ashen. Then she began to sway. Cathie reacted first, jumping up and catching her as she collapsed. "All for nothing," Jennet said in a barely audible voice before she fell silent.

CHAPTER TWENTY THREE

What did Jennet mean, "All for nothing?" Hannah asked herself the question over and over as she waited outside Dr. Carl Kaser's office. Jennet's reaction seemed very peculiar... excessive already. After all, she was financially well off and at the peak of her career. She certainly didn't need the money.

The doctor was inside examining Jennet, and had asked them to wait. Luckily, his office was next door to the law offices and he had seen his last patient when Cathie had run over to ask him to look at Jennet.

Peter briefly examined her after she collapsed and thought she'd only fainted, but as he said, he was a dentist, not a physician. When she didn't come to right away, Peter thought she should be seen by Dr. Kaser, and carried her into his office. He was still with her.

Kaitlin was nowhere in sight. In the excitement of Jennet's collapse, Hannah hadn't seen her leave, but according to what Peter told them, she didn't live too far away. She could easily walk home.

Had Jennet killed Nettie? Her words as she collapsed were incriminating, and she had reasons enough, Hannah had to admit. There was the matter of the inheritance. Maybe Jennet thought she'd inherit, or that Kaitlin would, now that Bob was out of the picture. That was only one of the motives. There was another even more compelling one: Jen might think Kaitlin was being abused by either Nettie or by Bob, with Nettie looking the other way. Then, there was Nettie's finagling Jennet's share of Doc Hope's money away from her. It was plain to Hannah that Jen resented Nettie, despite her protestations that she was only hurt, not angry.

The motives were there, all right, but how had Jennet Hope managed to kill Nettie when she was hundreds of miles away? Could she have hired someone? Hannah hoped maybe Carrie's investigator fellow - the one with the funny name, Jumbo or Jimbo - would turn something up. Leastwise they'd know if Jennet herself could have gotten back to Lancaster County, Hannah thought.

Carrie had gone back to her office to call Ian, who was supposed to be back at her place after the internment.

When it came to motives, nobody had one like Bob Adams. Only thing was, Hannah reasoned, he didn't know his wife had left everything to him. He was long gone by the time she changed her will. What did the old will say? Hannah wondered. Might be interesting to know.

Peter came out of the examining room alone. "Jennet's conscious now. Dr. Kaser thinks it's only emotional exhaustion, but he wants to put her in the hospital and run a few tests, just to be on the safe side."

"I think that is a good idea," Hannah said. "Peter, tell me, what did you hear Jen say just before she fainted?"

He ran his hand through his hair, as if it would jog his memory. "Damned if I remember, Hannah. I was so surprised by Annette's will, I wasn't paying much attention. I still don't get why she didn't leave anything to Kaitlin or Jennet. After what that bas...uh, blasted Bob Adams did to her, I found the will damn astonishing. As for Jen, I remember her mumbling something, then down she went. Why do want to know?"

"Just curious, Peter, just curious."

"Did Kate leave?" he asked, looking around.

"I guess; I have not seen her since we came over here with Jennet," Hannah answered.

"I should find her. Sort of tough on the kid, being left out of her mother's will completely. She's gotta be hurt."

Hannah thought hurt might not be the right word. Shocked maybe was more like it. "Go ahead, Peter. You do not have to stay here. Carrie will be right back and she called Ian, Jen's friend. We can handle things."

"Kaser wants her in Northside Community. Let me know how she's making out, okay?"

"Sure will," Hannah answered.

A few minutes later, Ian arrived with Carrie. He had changed clothes after the funeral, but Hannah thought Caroline's call must have interrupted him because he looked like he had finished dressing hastily. His sweater was buttoned crookedly. He looked worried, but in charge. After speaking briefly to the nurse, he was ushered into the examining room.

Several minutes later he came back into the waiting room." She says she's fine now, but I concur with the doctor. It's best she go to the hospital. She's agreed. He wants her to rest tonight; they'll run the tests tomorrow. He expects she'll be quite herself by then. I wouldn't worry." He sounds like he is trying to reassure himself more than us, Hannah thought.

"She will be fine, Ian." Hannah said.

"Quite." Ian said. "I'll stay until they send me home. If anything changes, I'll ring you. Otherwise I'll come along later."

"We'll be at the house all evening," Caroline said.

The sun was setting as they drove back to Caroline's. As they approached a ridge of hills, two Amish carriages with their high stepping horses were silhouetted against the sky. Such a peaceful picture, Hannah thought. No murder, no blackmail, no menace, no mystery. Thank the Lord. It made her think of her grandson, Josh, and his wedding coming up later in the week. Next to babies, weddings were Hannah's favorite events. She wasn't about to let a murder investigation put a damper on what should be a happy time for her family. She and Carrie were involved, no helping that; but she would keep it away from the family. Nothing was going to spoil Josh's wedding. Nothing, not even a murder. She sighed audibly.

What's wrong, Granny? Tired?" Caroline asked.

"A bit. I will be glad when things can get back to normal; when we find Nettie's murderer. The sooner we do, the sooner we can." She sat up straighter. "Carrie," she continued briskly as they drove on, "can I ask what was in Jennet's last will? Who inherited?"

"Officially, I'm not sure I should discuss it, Granny."

"You were not her lawyer then. Nor was Bryce. Right? Remember, this is a murder case, and it is your client who is dead."

"It would be a little hard to forget," Caroline said, sighing. "I suppose it's okay to talk to you about it. Bob still inherited the bulk of Nettie's estate, but there were substantial bequests to both Jennet and Kaitlin."

"I see," Hannah answered, wishing she really did see more than a murky mess.

"Why would she change to favor Bob when he took her money and left her?"

"She wanted him back, despite everything, I suppose. Who knows? She didn't say anything to me. I only wrote the will. I advised Nettie of the complications, but you know Nettie. She knew what she wanted," Caroline paused, thinking. "In retrospect, she did say one thing that seemed odd."

"That is?" Hannah asked, feeling like she was pulling teeth to get Carrie to open up.

"She asked me what would happen if Bob was already dead, or if he died before she did."

"That does not sound like such an odd question to me. So she was curious already."

"It was the way she asked, Gran. Her voice was so...um, calculating, like she had something in mind. And I was left with the strong impression that she detested him. Of course, he left her. That's reason enough to hate the guy. Especially when he cleaned out their joint bank account."

"Some hate - she left <u>him</u> all her money. Maybe she thought if he came back, she could keep him with money. After all, she was quite a few years older. He would probably outlive her. Meantime, she could make his life miserable. If anybody was capable of doing that, Nettie was the one. Strange, Carrie, these relationships between English men and English women are sure nothing like the Amish."

"Lucky for the Amish," Caroline commented, turning into her driveway.

Hannah had her ever present notebook out and had started making notes, despite the dim light. Caroline switched on the map light. "That is better," Hannah said. "Clever little gizmo. This book is starting to fill up, and I still have not, as the kids say, got a clue." She laughed ruefully. "By the way, as to the terms of the new will - what would happen if Bob had died before Nettie?"

"Kaitlin would inherit."

"Everything?"

"Yes, everything."

"You know, Carrie, it looks like we got more motives than crimes here. Everybody has got a good reason for wanting everybody else dead. It would be downright funny if this was a play. Would be a good farce. Instead, it is anything but funny.

"I sure do need to talk to Jennet," Hannah said, turning off the map light and closing her book. "Guess there is nothing I can do about that right now. In the meantime, I want to go back to Nettie's house. Would not hurt to search The Flying Needles, either."

"As it happens," Caroline said, "I want to start making inventories of both places. Tomorrow soon enough for you, Granny?"

CHAPTER TWENTY FOUR

When Caroline took Hannah home, she went in with her. Josh's wedding was in a few days, and Hannah was finishing still another quilt as a special present for the bride and groom. As in English families, the bride's family was responsible for the wedding and the feast which followed it. Amish weddings were enormous affairs, their size being limited only by how many people could be packed into one of their homes. Since all homes were "convertible" as Hannah liked to call it - with movable walls to accommodate church services, it was not unusual to see 300-400 people at a wedding. It was also an all day affair.

As Caroline and Hannah entered, the main house was quiet except for a bustle coming from the kitchen. The aroma of freshly baked cookies wafted out, filling the air with mouth watering anticipation. In the large room, the sideboard was piled high with cooling racks of apple-nut cookies. The counter was laden with a dozen cake pans, each greased and floured, ready for batter. In the morning, Caroline's mother and sister would mix and bake Rebecca's special coconut cakes to be frosted later and taken to Maria Schuler, the bride's mother. Although it wasn't required, relatives and close friends usually helped supply some of the food for the wedding guests. As mother of the groom, Rebecca was making a special effort to help with the long awaited event.

Hannah felt a little guilty when she saw all the work Rebecca had gone to without a bit of help from her. She was too busy with Nettie's murder to pitch in like she usually did. Lucky there were no babies to be delivered, or Rebecca would never have had time to accomplish so much. Now that Bethany was getting older, she was getting to be a big help to her mother, but it wasn't right to expect a ten-year-old to completely take over a grown woman's work.

"Hiya there," Rebecca greeted them. "I just now sent Bethany out to help her dad. You two eaten yet?" Rebecca was standing at the sideboard, where she was starting to pack the cooled cookies into very modern Tupperware containers. She popped a cookie into her mouth. Rebecca was as slim as a girl. Hannah wondered how she stayed that way as she was always snacking, or <u>fresching</u> as the Pennsylvania Dutch say.

"Yah," Hannah answered. "We stopped at Taco Bell on the way home". Most Amish are very fond of fast food, although they quickly adapt the latest specialties to be prepared at home where it is more frugal to indulge a large family. Feeding eight or nine people at McDonalds or Taco Bell could add up quickly.

Rebecca scooped some cookies on to a plate. "Have dessert then, and tell me about your day." She plopped into a chair, and looked eagerly at them. "What is going on? I know that look, Granny Hanny. You are in the middle of something already. Am I right?"

I must be transparent as a pane of glass, Hannah thought. Not a good quality for a detective. I will have to work on looking innocent.

Knowing she'd keep a confidence, Caroline and Hannah told Rebecca about the incredible day they had, beginning with their visit to Aggie, and ending with Jennet's departure for the hospital.

"<u>Gott in Himmel</u>!" Rebecca exclaimed. "What is going on? This used to be a peaceful place. Now we've got ourselves murder and blackmail and switched moms. Did I forget anything? Ah, yah, runaway husbands, and hysterical people right and left. The things the English get themselves into…" She shook her head, a troubled look on her face.

"Guess they can't help themselves," Hannah said. For reasons she didn't understand, she was always jumping in to defend the English. Maybe it was because several of her grandchildren had "gone English." Hannah was disappointed, but not surprised, since two out of every ten young people left the Amish. Her grandchildren, those who did leave the Amish, like Carrie, were turning out real well. That was a comfort, Hannah rationalized.

She thought of the few instances of Amish murder. There was Sarahjane Stoltzfus over in Yoder's church district who shot her husband with rifle the neighbors kept for scaring off foxes. Then there was Joseph Aaron King up the country - killed his wife back a year or so ago. Both of them were mentally ill, heard voices and such. Otherwise, violence, like adultery and divorce, was practically unheard of in the Amish population.

Later, in Hannah's house, now well lit from four large lanterns hung over her quilt frame, she and Caroline put the finishing touches on the last of Josh and Susannah's wedding quilts. It was the most traditional of Amish patterns, Sunshine and Shadows. Susannah herself had selected it, choosing the more modern colors of peach, apricot and amber over the older choices of deep jewel tones. Hannah found stitching traditional patterns was a relaxing change from the original and modern designs and techniques she usually did.

She was pleased Caroline was quilting again. Carrie made the most incredibly perfect stitches, like Hannah herself. Not surprising, as Hannah had taught her. When Rebecca had been so ill, bedridden much of the time following her series of miscarriages and Caroline was a small girl, Hannah had been more of a mother than Rebecca had been able to be. She taught her granddaughter everything she knew.

Despite that, Caroline always wanted to know more. Hannah wasn't a bit surprised Caroline's intellectual curiosity was the wedge that split her away from the Amish and into the English world. Eight years of Amish schooling only whetted Caroline's appetite for more education. Unlike Hannah, Caroline wasn't content with books from the library. No, she had to sample the outside world, and once she did, she was there to stay.

Now she was back in Lancaster County and, if not Amish anymore, at least to Hannah's way of thinking Carrie was the next best thing. She came back to help her people deal with the increasingly invasive world they tried so hard to separate themselves from. Between the tourists and the developers, it was becoming more and more difficult to do that. They needed empathetic help, and as Hannah looked at Carrie, placidly stitching, she knew they'd found the right person in her granddaughter. Hannah never doubted God had a plan. Carrie, leaving the Amish only to be here now to help, was definitely part of it.

But not for a minute did she think God had any part in Nettie Adams' death. That wasn't God, Hannah thought; that was man with his free will, gone wrong...gone real wrong.

Now she'd gotten herself right smack dab in the middle of righting that wrong, not that it could bring poor Nettie back. The best that Hannah could do was help catch the murderer and keep the same thing from happening to somebody else. Maybe Chief Benton wasn't so far wrong at first when he jumped to the conclusion that Bob Adams might have killed his wife. "Bob sure would profit by Nettie's death...all that money," Hannah said aloud, breaking the quiet in the room. "He sure better have the world's best alibi if he does show up. Yes, sir, I would indeed like to know where Bob Adams is right this minute."

"And where he was when Nettie was killed," Caroline added, taking her final stitch and putting her needle in the pincushion. "Well, Granny, it's been relaxing. Heavens knows, both of us needed a break, but I want to get home. I want to see if Jimbo called, and I still need to talk to Molly and Stephen tonight."

"Okay," Hannah said, getting up. "When do we get going in the morning?"

"Eight too early for you?"

"Even earlier is fine," Hannah answered. "We have no time to waste. The wedding is Thursday. It would be good to have this over by then. Then we would have even more to celebrate."

"Are you ever the optimist!" Caroline said, her look betraying her disbelief.

"Never hurts to look for the sunshine, Carrie," Hannah said. She didn't add what she was thinking: even if all she really saw was shadows aplenty.

CHAPTER TWENTY FIVE

When Caroline got home, Ian was already there. He said Dr. Kaiser had given Jennet a sedative and it was pointless to stay with her since she'd sleep all night. He planned to return to the hospital by seven the next morning when she was scheduled to have her tests.

"I brought you a bottle of brandy, Caroline. I don't know about you, but I've had quite a day. Do you mind?" Ian asked.

"No, not at all. I'll even join you, although I'm not much of a drinker, Ian. I usually stick to wine."

"The Amish don't drink, do they?" Ian asked as he watched Caroline get glasses down.

"No, although I've seen homemade wines for medicinal purposes. And occasionally, an Amish boy out raising the devil, or in his rumpaspringa period as it's called, gets drunk and has to be disciplined. Last week I was called in to defend one, Sammy Aaron Lapp. He'd gotten drunk, and fallen asleep while driving his souped-up buggy. And his was a real piece of work...even had a stereo. Anyway, he'd run into a parked car. He refused bail, because according to Sammy, 'I did not run into anything; the horse did.'"

Ian laughed. "What happened to the lad?"

"I convinced him the county jail was no place to be; his family needed him at home. It gave him a face-saving reason to make bail. He'll probably get a suspended sentence and a fine. I think Sammy Aaron's dad will figure the boy has had enough rumpaspringa for a while and keep him close to home. The Amish are very lenient with their teenage boys. They want them to get the wildness out of their systems before they join the church."

"When do they do that?" Ian asked.

"Oh, anywhere from seventeen to the early twenties. They have to join before they marry, so that's a real incentive. It's the same for girls, except they aren't allowed the freedom boys have."

She poured brandy into Ian's snifter and a few drops into her own. After they were sitting in the living room, she decided now was a good time to ask him a few questions. "Ian, what did Jennet say when she got to the hospital?"

"Really not much of anything. She said she was sorry for worrying us and she was quite all right. I'd say she was feeling rather embarrassed about fainting."

"How well do you know Jen?"

"We met in London a couple of years ago. I must admit, I was rather taken with her immediately. I'm afraid I made rather a mess of it," he said, managing to look uncharacteristically sheepish, and charming all at the same time.

"How was that?" Caroline encouraged.

"I took her to dinner and things seem to be going along quite swimmingly. Then she had to go on to Paris and Milan for the spring fashion openings. I had to go to India so it was a month or so before I rang her up. She was in New York, and a few days before I called, I decided to send this quite ostentatious lot of flowers to her at her office....Quite bad taste on my part...I don't know whatever possessed me..." Ian looked puzzled, as if he couldn't see the obvious. Caroline tried not to smile. "At any rate, she didn't mention the flowers, nor has she to this day. She must have been quite mortified and thought I was a ridiculous chap."

"How many flowers did you send, Ian?"

"Uhm...twenty-four, uhm ...dozen roses," Ian said, studying the floor. "Long stemmed."

"I see. That is a lot of flowers. It's also incredibly romantic."

"Quite," Ian said. "But not the sort of thing you send to someone's office. It was a dreadful faux pas. Perhaps if I had sent them to Jennet's apartment..."

"Well, you seem to have made up for any misunderstanding. You appear to be very good friends now," Caroline said.

"More than that, Caroline. I've asked Jennet to marry me."

"That's wonderful, Ian," Caroline said enthusiastically.

"Let's hope so. She hasn't said yes, yet. I certainly wouldn't dream of pressing her for an answer now. She needs some time, given all that's going on. She's been under a lot of strain for the past few months. Her job is very stressful and I know Annette has drained her."

"What do you mean?"

"Oh, after her husband ran off, Nettie was constantly on the telephone to Jennet, ringing her up at all hours to talk."

"I see," Caroline said. "Have you heard what happened regarding the will?"

"Jennet said her sister left everything to that husband."

"That's right," Caroline answered. She swirled the amber liquid in her glass. "Did she expect that? Or didn't you two talk about it?"

"Actually, we did discuss it, Caroline. Jennet didn't expect to inherit. She expected Kaitlin would. I'm sure it was a surprise to hear that Adams scoundrel was left everything, but I don't think Jennet was so shocked she collapsed because of it. I'd say it was only a coincidence. She was overwrought, exhausted, and very fragile. The will was simply, as they say in Egypt, the straw that broke the camel's back."

"How did Jennet feel about Nettie?"

Ian was sitting back in his chair, eyes half closed. "Ambivalent would be the word I'd choose to describe her feelings. Annette didn't have exactly a sterling character. Jennet is too good, too nice. Anyone else wouldn't have put up with the way Annette treated her. Jennet simply turned the other cheek. Actually, Nettie didn't deserve to have such a loving sister. I might be prejudiced, but..." Ian sat up and focused his expressive eyes directly at Caroline. "Jennet is a wonderful person, Caroline. She would never hurt anyone, least of all her twin."

Well, what did she expect, Caroline thought after Ian excused himself to go to bed? He was, as Granny had warned her, besotted with Jennet. If she was an axe murderer holding onto the axe with it still dripping blood, Ian wouldn't be able to see it. Ah, love. How it colors one's perceptions.

Inexplicably, she thought of Stephen. She'd promised to call him. First, she wanted to check her messages, something she hadn't wanted to do with Ian listening. The light on her machine flashed and the indicator said she had two messages waiting. As it whirred to rewind, she finished the last of her brandy. She realized for the first time how tired she was.

"Hi, Carrie..I mean Caroline," Stephen's deep, and, Caroline thought, rather sexy, voice greeted her. Maybe it was the brandy. Or something. She found it kind of touching the way he tried so hard to call her Caroline, not the Amish "Carrie", the name he'd first known her by. "Call me, soonest. I'm still at the store and I'm anxious to know what's happening." The machine's date stamp said he'd called an hour ago.

The next message began. "Hiya Caroline. How ya doin?" It was the hearty voice of Jimbo Johnson, the New York investigator she'd contacted to check out Jennet. "Your gal is clean. Story checks out. Call for details. I turn in about midnight. Anytime up to then's good. Otherwise, talk to ya manana. Oh, yeah, I Fedexed the tapes we talked about." Jimbo was sending the tapes he'd managed to get of Jennet's shows. Caroline wasn't really sure herself why she'd wanted them. Something in the back of her mind told her to look at them. Maybe Jennet had recorded her shows in advance or repeated them. In any case they were on the way. When she and Hannah were going to find the time or the opportunity to watch them was a good question.

It looked like Jennet couldn't have killed Nettie. Unless she'd hired someone. Caroline couldn't buy that. It was possible, but unless Jennet Hope was the world's best actress, or a nut case, Caroline believed her innocent.

There was a soft knock at the door. Caroline glanced at her watch. It wasn't even nine o'clock. It seemed much later. She went to the door and peered out the peephole. Stephen stood on the other side making a face at her.

She opened the door. "Hi. I was just about to call you. What a day I have had!" She stood aside for Stephen to enter.

"Sorry, I should have called. But you were on my way, and I just figured..." Stephen said, looking awkward. He was wearing jeans and an Irish fisherman's sweater. Only men who look that good in jeans should wear them, Caroline thought. What had those few sips of brandy done to her? Or could she blame the liquor?

"It's okay, Fen," Caroline said, forgetting herself and calling him her pet name for him from years ago. "I'm glad to see you."

Stephen looked puzzled. "You are?"

Oh hell, she said to herself. Why fight this? And she went into his arms. It felt wonderful and absolutely right. He didn't ask questions, but held her as gently as if she were one of Molly's collection dolls he was afraid would break.

"Caroline..." Stephen murmured into her hair, and tightened his grip on her. She could feel the furious pounding of his heart. Or was it her own heart beating so hard?

"It's all right, Fen, you can call me Carrie," she said, reaching up to kiss him.

CHAPTER TWENTY SIX

Hannah wasn't surprised when Caroline told her over coffee at Hannah's house about Stephen's visit the previous evening. Her intuition had told her it would only be a matter of time before Carrie would own up to her feelings for Stephen. Now it had happened. Hannah couldn't be more pleased despite Caroline's protestations that she wasn't ready to re-marry Stephen. That would happen too, Hannah was sure. She loved seeing that look on her favorite granddaughter's face. Carrie was in love, and Hannah was delighted.

"I made us a picnic lunch, so we would not have to stop," Hannah said, gathering up a basket as they prepared to leave for the Adams' house.

"Good. Stephen offered to bring us lunch, too. But I told him you'd probably have something fixed," Caroline said. "I have to leave around two o'clock. Today is Molly's mother-daughter Brownie meeting. Poor little kid; I've been spending so little time with her lately. If I didn't show up, both of us would be disappointed. I'll be back about four if we aren't finished by then." Caroline got her keys out of her pocket. "Stephen said he'd be over late this afternoon to help."

"Good. I doubt if we will finish even today; it is a big house. I want to take my time. We cannot afford to be slipshod in this investigation. I want to read every scrap of paper in the place and search every nook and cranny. In other words, go over it extra carefully. We can use Stephen's help; sometimes men are useful... something might need moving or lifting," Hannah said, looking at Caroline to see if she'd get a reaction from her granddaughter..

Carrie didn't disappoint her. "Granny! You chauvinist!"

"Just stating facts," Hannah said. "Did not mean anything personal. Stephen Brown has a good mind as well as a strong back. I have a feeling we will need all of both we can get. By the way, what are you going to do about Flying Needles? Too bad Nettie's store has to be sold. She told me it was turning a good profit."

"That's the one thing that might help find a buyer; it was making money. Nettie pretty much single handedly ran the place, except for Sadie and Annie. As I understood it, all they did was repair quilts."

"Believe they did take over when Nettie was away - on a buying trip, that kind of thing. I do not imagine Nettie would have let them in on the business details. She did not care for those two much. Besides, she liked to run her own show," Hannah said.

"Well, they can help with the inventory if they want to."

"Oh, I would just bet they want to. Did you see the look on Sadie's face yesterday at the funeral home when she could not find out about the burial plans? I suppose I was rude not to answer, but they knew it was family only. They were not invited. They just have to be in the thick of things yet. Sadie is bad enough with her snooping and Annie is getting more peculiar by the day."

"On second thought, I'm not sure if I want them inventorying the store, despite their knowledge of quilts. Granny..how about you?"

"I do not know, Carrie. Let us get the house finished first. That is daunting enough for a start," Hannah answered.

"I wonder if Flying Needles will be so profitable without Nettie. She was the cog that turned the wheel."

"Ach, Carrie, you are using clichés, already." Hannah couldn't resist teasing Carrie on one of her rare slips into clichés.

"I'm glad you recognize one when you hear it, Gran. You're improving," Caroline shot back.

"We have no time for funning," Hannah said, serious now, her mind back on Nettie's murder. "We better get over to Nettie's. I have a nasty feeling it is going to be a long day."

By mid-day, Caroline and Hannah had carefully searched and inventoried most of the main floor of the Adams' house. Caroline was using a video tape recorder which helped with the general inventory. The searching took longer.

"I was right about Nettie keeping all of her business papers here at home, and not at the shop," Hannah said, as she searched through the contents of still another file from Nettie's den. "Too bad she did not get a computer. It would make both your job and mine," Hannah commented to Caroline. She spread the contents of a file cabinet on Nettie's inlaid wood dining room table, which had been covered with a sheet to protect it.

"Not yours, Granny. You wouldn't be able to work on the computer. It is forbidden for you. Then I'd be doing that, too. For some reason, Nettie didn't like computers, or simply hadn't gotten around to it."

Hannah studied the latest records. "I am getting a picture of Nettie's life, and it is sure confusing. Mostly, she was as tight with her money as could be, but once in awhile she made a generous gesture."

Caroline looked up from where she was taping Nettie's extensive collection of china. "What kind of generous gestures do you mean, Gran?"

"Well, there is this quilt she bought from Connie King. You know Connie; she's one of God's special children." That was how the Amish referred to the mentally impaired and physically challenged in their community. Whenever possible, the Amish tried to let the person live as normal a life as possible.

"Connie makes quilts?" Caroline asked, surprise in her voice.

"She tries. And it looks like Nettie bought one. Here is a notation, neatly printed in Nettie's ledger. She paid exactly what she paid for the other King women's quilts."

"I guess Nettie had her soft side after all. Lots of people are inconsistent."

"Are you sure you don't mind being here alone, Gran?" Caroline asked as she got ready to leave a little before two o'clock. "The police aren't patrolling the property any longer."

"I will be just fine, Carrie," Hannah answered as she walked Caroline to the door. "Now that we know how to work the alarm, I will activate it when you leave; I will be snug as a bug in a rug here for a couple of hours. Go, or you will be late. Give Molly a hug for me, and tell her I will see her at Josh's wedding."

"Okay, Gran, if you're sure…"

"I am very sure. Go already," Hannah said, practically closing the door in Caroline's face.

Half an hour later, Hannah had finished the downstairs. Almost a day gone, and not much to show for it she thought. She and Caroline determined that Nettie was probably worth somewhere in the neighborhood of a million dollars, even after the thousands Bob took with him. Rich as Nettie was, it sure had not made her very happy. Hannah thought of Nettie and Jennet as small girls. It saddened her to think of what had become of them. Here Nettie was dead, and Jennet in the hospital and very troubled.

Going to the kitchen, Hannah looked up the phone number of Northside Community Hospital and dialed it. "I would like to speak to Jennet Hope, please," she told the operator.

"I'm sorry, Ma'am, she is not receiving calls," the operator said, crisply. "You will have to speak to her doctor."

Doctor Kaser's answering service said they were out until the morning, but she could leave a message. She didn't.

Another call to Caroline's condominium produced only Carrie's answering machine's announcement. Maybe Ian was at the hospital and she could have him paged. She dialed the hospital. "Please ring the nurse's desk on Jennet Hope's floor,"

Hannah asked. The nurse at the desk wouldn't tell her anything about Jennet's condition, saying only she had orders not to give out information, and referring Hannah to Dr. Kaser's office again. When she asked for Ian, the nurse said he had left. So much for information gathering. Guess I have no choice except to wait, Hannah thought. There are times I wish I was English and could just hop in my car and drive wherever I wanted to go. I'd run over to that hospital and see what was going on for myself.

She stood at the long windows in the breakfast room which looked out onto Nettie Adams' back yard. The unfinished pool and the pool house interlaced by concrete walkways gave the place a vital, work-in-progress, look as if something important was taking place. It was a warm, sunny day with only a hint of a breeze. Hannah suddenly felt the need for some of that fresh air to clear her mind before she faced the upstairs.

She carefully deactivated the alarm, then let herself out with the key, resetting the box from outside. "Lot of trouble," she mumbled out loud. Robbery was getting to be an ever increasing problem, even for the Amish. Several Amish families had their homes rifled when they were away at church. It was thought the intruders were looking for some of the antique Amish quilts which sold for up to $25,000 to collectors. There sure wasn't much else to steal that would be resalable...no electronic gear, that was for sure. Everybody knew the Amish were away at church for most of the day every other Sunday. Their homes were easy targets. Lots of Amish now kept a big dog in the house to guard things, and nobody kept real valuable old quilts at home. The Amish had to resort to oversized lock boxes to store their heirloom quilts. It was yet another reason why so many of the Amish of Lancaster County were moving to more rural areas. Hannah, for the first time in her life had begun to lock her own house. She hated the thought that it had become necessary.

She walked around the yard, following the paths and concrete areas to keep her black Reeboks out of the mud. Here and there, frost blackened flowers sagged forlornly against the house. In spite of the sunny day, a faint, smoke-like smell of fall was in the air. Hannah heard far away honking of geese bound for the South. The wind was playing games. The breeze, so gentle at first, now picked up and whipped into a biting wind. Hannah gathered her black cloak more tightly around her. Still, it was invigorating to be outdoors rather than in Nettie's beautiful, lifeless house.

The pool house stood boarded up at the far end of the empty unfinished swimming pool. It was a multi-roomed affair, designed to also act as a self-contained guest house. That part was pretty much finished with the walls and roof done. Hannah had seen the plans for the completed structure. It would have been grand with its glass enclosed "Florida Room." She wondered what they called such rooms in Florida? Surely not "Pennsylvania Rooms."

She peered in between the boards across the window. Cracks of light from the windows opposite cast shadows on the dusty plywood sub-floors, making them look striped. The room appeared empty except for a large credenza covered in plastic in the middle of the room. Curious to see the inside, Hannah tried the door. It was locked. She tried the house key and it worked. The door swung open and Hannah stepped inside.

Later, she'd remember how cold it was inside. And how surprised she was when something hit her from behind. Then she fell into warm, dreamless darkness.

CHAPTER TWENTY SEVEN

Caroline and Stephen arrived at Nettie's almost simultaneously. After she had taken Molly to Stephen's and left her in the care of his housekeeper, she'd returned to the Adams' house. Before she had time to get out of her seat belt, Stephen drove up in his van, jumped out, and came over to her car.

"Hi, Love," he said, all the awkwardness between them now gone.

"Hi, Fen," Caroline answered, her heart lurching at the mere sound of the word 'love' from him.

He leaned down and gave her a quick kiss. "Granny might be watching. She's going to tease us enough. I supposed you told her."

"Of course. She'd guess anyway. I look too happy."

"Good," Stephen answered, as she got out of the car. "Me, too." Hand in hand, they walked to the front door and rang the bell. There was no answer.

Ten minutes later, Stephen broke the glass in the kitchen door, setting off the ear splitting alarm. Once inside, a by now thoroughly worried Caroline deactivated it.

"Granny!" she called. "Where are you?" With Stephen close behind her, she searched every room on the first floor, then did the same to the rest of the house. There was no sign of Hannah anywhere.

"Her purse is right there, Stephen," Caroline said, pointing to the hall. "She wouldn't have gone far without it."

Stephen was studying the alarm panel. "Carrie, when you turned the alarm off, was it set like it would be for someone inside, or completely activated?"

"God, Fen, I don't remember."

"Think!" Stephen ordered.

She closed her eyes, trying to remember. She willed herself to be calm, despite a pounding head. "The light was on. It was completely set. That means Granny must have gone out and set it."

"Right, but where would she go without her purse? Maybe she walked home for something, just forgot her purse. She isn't getting forgetful is she?"

"Absolutely not. Let me see if her house keys are in her bag." They were. "She must have a key to this house with her. The dead bolts were all on."

"Let's search the grounds," Stephen said, taking charge and sounding completely calm. "Maybe she went for a walk. She could have gone to the Shoops. If we don't find her here, call over there."

"I know she felt kind of badly about ignoring Sadie at the funeral," Caroline said. Stephen looked puzzled. "I forgot you, weren't there. I'll tell you about it later. Maybe she did go over there. I'll run in to the house and give them a call. Keep calling her out here. If she isn't at the Shoops..." Caroline broke off, not really knowing what she would do next. Let her be at Sadie and Annie's, she prayed silently.

Caroline picked up the phone in the kitchen. The redial button! If Hannah had gone somewhere, maybe she called first. Caroline pressed the button. "Northside Community Hospital," a voice announced. Perhaps Ian had stopped by and taken Granny to see Jen. That would explain Hannah's absence. Except for her purse...it was still in the hall. Maybe she <u>had</u> forgotten it; Ian had that kind of effect on her. Caroline smiled at the thought. That had to be it.

"May I speak to Jennet Hope's room, please?"

"The patient was just discharged," the operator answered.

"She was? Do you know where she went?" Caroline was more than a little surprised.

"She was discharged; I have no further information."

"Thank you," Caroline answered, then dialed her own number. All she got was her recording.

The scenario she was hoping for, that Hannah had gone to visit Jen, evaporated. Jen wasn't even at the hospital. Besides, as Caroline's logic returned, she knew Hannah would never have left her purse, failed to leave Caroline and Stephen a note when she knew they were due, or locked them out.

She called her father's dairy farm. Amish businesses were permitted to have telephones as long as they weren't in the house. Her father, Daniel, answered after several rings. He was slightly out of breath.

"Daat," Caroline said, keeping her voice steady. She didn't want to worry her family unnecessarily. "Is Gran around, by any chance?"

"Why, no, Carrie. I thought she was with you today." Daniel sounded surprised.

"She was. I had to go to Molly's school..." she paused, not knowing what to say so as not to alarm her father. "When I got back she wasn't here."

"Wohl, Carrie. You know Granny. She is always too antsy to do nothing but wait. Most likely she is out walking. You are not worried are you?"

"No, just checking, that's all."

"She will turn up, Carrie. If I see her, I will have her call," Daniel answered, assuming Caroline was at home. He hung up without saying goodbye. Sometimes Amish telephone manners could be improved, Caroline thought. Unused to using the phone, the Amish often dispensed with hello and goodbye.

Quickly, she looked up the Shoop number and dialed it. There was no answer after ten rings.

Stephen came into the kitchen as she hung up. "Oh, God, Fen. I never should have left her alone here. What if...?" Caroline couldn't finish her sentence. It was too awful to say aloud. What if the murderer came back? What if he hurt Hannah?

Stephen put comforting arms around her. "Come on, Carrie, don't borrow trouble. Remember what Granny Hanny herself says, the interest is too high."

As Stephen must have known it would, quoting Granny calmed Caroline down. "You're right, Stephen. I'm getting upset over nothing. It isn't like me to lose my perspective. She probably simply went out for a walk; it's a gorgeous day. We'll find her. We'll keep looking. Let's try outside again."

They circled the property, Caroline going one way, Stephen the other, both of them calling for Hannah. Silence was their only answer. "Fen I don't see any footprints. It's muddy around here. If Granny had taken a walk in the back, there would be footprints. There are tire tracks, lots of them, but no footprints."

"I noticed the same thing. She would have had to stay on the paths or taken the road. Both the garage and that building at the end of the pool are locked. I looked in the windows, but I don't see anyone. Do you have keys?"

"No. The only key we've found is the one Granny has. There must be others, but we haven't found them yet."

"I don't want to waste time looking for them, Carrie. I'll have to break more windows." They were standing by the garage where bricks were stacked several feet high in preparation for building a wall. Steven picked up a brick. "Stand back, Carrie," he said, breaking the glass in the side door. It shattered noisily, falling on the cement. He reached in and opened the door. "Nettie should have had key-only dead bolts installed. Anyone can get in this way."

"Lucky for us. We'd have a hard time squeezing in the window," Caroline said, kicking broken glass out of her way. She was trying to keep calm, taking deep breaths and remembering how intelligent and quick witted her grandmother was.

"I don't see anyone," Stephen said. The garage echoed emptily. Nettie's van was parked outside, and since Nettie's death, no one had bothered to put it in the garage. Inside, it was neat, and except for a faint oil stain where Nettie usually parked, looked almost unused. Long cupboards lined one wall. They weren't deep enough to hide a person, even one Hannah's size, but Stephen opened each anyway. Tools, mostly for the yard, were carefully arranged. Other yard tools were stored at one end.

"Nothing here," Stephen said.

Caroline was relieved and increasingly worried all at the same time. The longer Hannah was missing, the worse the consequences could be. "The only place left to look is the pool house. But I don't know why she'd go in there," Caroline said. Let's go, and, Stephen, bring a brick."

CHAPTER TWENTY EIGHT

The dank, wet smell of earth was the first thing Hannah was aware of. A pervasive cold permeated her consciousness. Gott in Himmel was her first thought, I am buried alive!

She tried to open her eyes. At first she thought she was blind. Then she realized all her senses were distorted by the dark and the cold. Gradually, she took stock. Something was across her eyes, roughly digging into her face, preventing her from seeing, gouging hairpins into her scalp beneath her bonnet and prayer cap. Her bonnet was pressed so tightly into her ears, she couldn't hear anything but the sound of her own heart beating erratically. A gag was stuffed uncomfortably into her mouth, making it hard even to swallow. She couldn't cry out nor move her tongue. Beginning at the shoulder, she was trussed like a turkey, her wrists tied together chest high with a piece of cord. Her ankles were also tightly bound. With every attempt to move, tongues of fiery pain licked at the back of her head. She must have been hit over the head. Someone had hit her and put her in this place. Someone who wanted her dead. And someone too much of a coward to kill her outright.

The <u>dumbassel</u>, she said, using her most potent swearword, leaving me here to die. Anger and adrenaline energized her. Her hands were bound in front of her. Whoever put her here was an amateur, too lazy, or in too much of a hurry, to move her heavy cape to get her hands behind her. Or maybe he figured she'd die before she had a chance of getting loose. Hannah tried moving a little. Having no idea where she was lying, she was fearful to advance much. What if she was on a hill, or at the edge of a hole? She wiggled a little, trying to ignore the searing pain in her head. The only parts of her body she could move were her fingers. They may be enough, she thought, hope glimmering through the darkness of her prison.

She took inventory of her clothing. Her heavy cloak was wadded up under her, exposing her dress covered by the omnipresent apron. Carefully, she worked her fingers, supple from so much quilting, together, and pulled at the material of her apron. She was trying to get at the sturdy, long straight pins which fastened the front of every Amish woman's dress. The ones Hannah used were as strong as hatpins. It was slow, tedious going. The greasy smell of her gag was making her feel nauseous. That's all she'd need, Hannah thought, to throw up and choke to death. Suddenly, she was aware of a sound. Oh no, her would-be killer had returned to see if she was dead! Or to finish the job. She lay perfectly still, not daring to breathe.

"Hannah, Granny Hanny." It was Stephen's voice. Hannah struggled to call out, to make some noise. It was hopeless. The foul smelling gag was wedged so hard in her mouth, she couldn't do much more than utter a muffled croak. Stephen called again, closer still.

She must be somewhere at Nettie's house. What had happened? Her memory was fuzzy. She had been exploring the pool house. Someone must have hit her, that's why her head hurt so, and put her under the floor boards in the crawl space. That's where she must be. She heard Carrie's voice, urgently joining Stephen's in calling for her. Again, Hannah tried to make a sound. Nothing. She wiggled as much as she could hoping to find something to hit, but the irregular dirt floor and her bonds kept her from moving.

She resumed working her way towards the pins. If she could reach the point of one, she might be able to loosen the ropes on her wrist. It wasn't much of an idea, but the only thing she could think of to help herself. She wasn't about to lie here and die. Pricking herself, she found a long pin. Slowly, she edged the pin's sharp, strong point against the rope. The rope on her hands didn't seem to be too thick. Maybe, just maybe, she could loosen or fray it enough to slip a hand out. She heard Stephen and Carrie's voices, continuing to call her, coming closer. Now they sounded right overhead. Hannah tried again to make some noise. This time she could do no more than squeak ineffectually.

"We've gone over this whole place, Carrie," Stephen said. "She's not at her house, or at your folks'. I'm going to call the police." He sounded grim.

"All right, Stephen. Go ahead. Try to call Annie and Sadie again after you call the police. I have to do something. I know we've looked everywhere, but I'm going to keep looking. Maybe we missed something. I'll start in the house and work my way outside again."

Carrie sounds calm, Hannah thought, knowing action always calmed her granddaughter in a crisis. Like her, Carrie rarely fell apart in an emergency. She'd save the emotion for later.

I hope by the time Carrie checks the pool house again, I will be loose or Carrie and Stephen will think to lift up the floor boards.

Hannah worked faster at the tedious job of scratching the pin across the thin rope. She could feel threads coming loose from it. At all once, the pin bent. It was no use trying to straighten it. She painfully stretched her hands higher to see if she could reach the pin above, pressing her elbows into her sides to help them reach up a bit farther. Finally she caught the next pin and began the process anew. Each movement of her bound hands strained her arms painfully, grating them roughly against the ropes holding her body.

All at once, the rope around her wrists slackened; she'd broken enough threads to loosen it. Wiggling her hand around, she pulled one, then the other hand out of the rope. Now she could reach her gag. She wrenched the foul thing out, coughing. She pulled her blindfold off. Her eyes watered painfully when the light hit them. Small patches of late afternoon sun checkered the dirt from the vents on the west side of the building. Next she held perfectly still, listening to determine if anyone was coming. She wasn't going to waste her voice screaming until she heard Carrie or Stephen. Meantime, she'd work at her ropes. It took only a few minutes to slip an arm out by pulling with her hands. Soon she was free altogether and looking for a way out. There was no trap door, nor any escape hatch obvious from the crawlspace where she was trapped. She listened again, but still didn't hear anyone. Her best bet might be to knock the screen out of the air vents. Slight as she was, even she couldn't fit through one, but at least it would make it easier to be heard and maybe seen. All she needed was a tool. All around the dirt floor were discarded pieces of wood, most too small to do any good. Then she saw a longer piece, partly buried in the dirt. She crawled over to where it lay and tugged at it. It was stuck tight. Picking up a smaller pointed scrap, she began digging. Something was holding the larger piece fast. She starting digging with her hands to loosen it when something brightly colored showed against the dirt. It was a quilt. By the looks of it, an old Amish one. How the dickens did it get here, she wondered. She uncovered it further. Something seemed to be wrapped in it. She freed more of the quilt, unwrapping it at the same time. She lurched back. "Oh, my Gott, " Hannah

137

said aloud. She gazed in horror at a partly decomposed human hand. "There is a body in here!"

At that moment, she heard voices.

"Carrie! Stephen!" Hannah yelled at the top of her lungs. "I am in here... with a dead body."

CHAPTER TWENTY NINE

Stephen and Caroline heard Hannah's cries. It hadn't taken long for Stephen to find the trap door to the crawl space. A crate lay over it, obscuring its presence the first time they'd looked in the pool house. The minute Stephen had the trap door open, Hannah scrambled out on her own.

"I'm not spending any time I do not have to with a body," she cried, especially one in that condition."

Despite Hannah's vigorous insistence that she was fine and all she needed was some fresh air, Caroline took her to be seen by a doctor. After checking Hannah over, he pronounced her to be in surprisingly good shape. She had a lump on the back of her head, but layers of bonnet, prayer cap and thick hair had saved her from a more serious injury. Other than a few contusions from the ropes, she had no other injuries. Hannah insisted on returning to Nettie's house to learn what the police had found out about the body.

The coroner had taken away the body by the time Caroline and Hannah arrived back at the Adams' house. The police were now swarming over Nettie's looking for further evidence.

"We found identification in the victim's clothing," Chief Benton told them, as they sat at Nettie's kitchen table. "Until the coroner gets a positive make, this is unofficial, but could be you found Bob Adams," Benton said.

"I figured," Hannah said, as she crunched somewhat noisily on a hard candy. She complained to Caroline that she couldn't get rid of the taste of the gag, so they had stopped at a convenience store on the way back to pick up some mints. "That body had been there some months. And at least the hand looked to be about the right size for Bob Adams."

"It won't take long for the coroner to I.D. the body. He already sent for Adams' dental records," Benton said. "That will give us enough for now. The state lab can do DNA match later."

"Anything new on the APB for the man you have been hunting for in connection with Annette Adams' death, the one the Shoop sisters saw?" Hannah asked.

"Afraid not. We'll keep looking, don't you worry. He'll turn up sooner or later."

"Umm," Hannah said, chomping harder on the mint.

"Now, I don't want you to get the wrong idea. I'm not saying this guy the Shoop ladies saw is positively the perp, uh, Mrs. Adams' killer. He just looks like a likely candidate. I'm keeping an open mind," Benton said.

"That why you were at the Adams' funeral behind the curtains in the family viewing area?" Hannah asked.

"You are very observant, Mrs. Miller. How did you know it was me?"

"A careful investigator always goes to the murder victim's funeral. He can note who is there, and their reactions," Hannah answered.

"I was half expecting Bob Adams to show up," Benton said.

"Guess he did that, if not at Nettie's services," Hannah said dryly.

"Yeah, now I got another killing on my hands," Benton said.

Caroline was wondering if Benton thought the two murders were connected, or if he still thought the man seen in the Shoops' yard was Nettie's murderer, and someone else was Bob's. She knew he wouldn't be likely to speculate to them. Or would he? She could try. "What did the State Police Lab come up with on Annette Adams' death?" Caroline asked.

"So far, not much to help us find the killer. The weapon was a common butcher knife, the kind sold everywhere. Far as we can tell, it wasn't from in there." He pointed to the Adams' kitchen. "The deceased had real fancy knives in a rack, all still there."

"What does that tell you, Chief?" Hannah asked.

"How do you mean?"

"Does it seem likely to you that an itinerant person like you think killed Nettie would carry a large butcher knife along with him? Would he stop to wipe prints off? Would he try to dispose of the weapon?"

"He might; who knows?" Benton shrugged his shoulders.

Who knows? Caroline thought. Obviously not our esteemed Acting Chief Benton. His cockiness was increasingly irritating. Like Hannah, she wasn't very fond of know-it-alls, especially when they didn't know much of anything at all.

"We got all kinds of hair samples," Benton said, sitting back and crossing one knee over the other leg. "When we find the killer, if we're lucky, we can match the D.N.A.; then we got him cold." Benton said.

"How about blood?" Hannah asked. "What turned up there?"

"Only the deceased's blood. There was nothing under her fingernails, either. It was like she ran, but didn't actually fight her attacker off... you know, hand-to-hand like. Usually in a knifing, there are little cuts on the victims' hands, where they tried to protect themselves. Not with Mrs. Adams; she must have been too scared. Maybe figured she could talk him out of it. Then he cornered her and plunged the knife in before she could react."

Caroline shuddered, thinking of the horror Nettie faced.

"What other findings do you have, Kiel Benton?" Hannah asked.

"We did the usual tests on the deceased for chemicals in her blood. I won't go into detail, but some of them take a while. We did get a blood alcohol on her, though. She hadn't been drinking. No, Nettie Adams was as sober as a judge."

Caroline saw a pained expression cross Hannah's face. She recognized her grandmother was seething. Caroline didn't think it was Benton's use of a cliché, either. It was routine to test a murder victim's blood for alcohol and chemicals, and Hannah knew it. Maybe it was Benton's supercilious tone of voice, as if Nettie's blood alcohol level was important in this case.

"Nettie never drank, Chief Benton. She was allergic to liquor," Hannah said. "Wasn't that in her medical records?"

Benton looked surprised. "I've been ... uh, sorta busy; haven't had time to study them," he said.

Caroline had seen the kind of look Benton had on his face before. It was the same way a witness who was evading telling the truth, but not wanting to lie, looked. I'd be willing to bet Benton didn't even think to get Nettie's medical records.

"What about the footprints?" Hannah asked.

"You know, that is weird," Benton said. "It looks from the measurements and the impressions we got both from here and the Shoop yard that the guy who made the footprints was wearing borrowed shoes, or something."

"What?" Hannah, Stephen, and Caroline all asked in unison.

141

"Yeah," Benton continued. "The print of the shoe, a work shoe, was size 12 ½, but the foot inside it was like more like an 8-9 ½. Somebody must have sore feet from wearing shoes that much too big." Benton leaned forward in his chair, playing to his now attentive audience. "I figure this guy was some bum who stole the shoes off of someone. I dunno, maybe he traded them for something or picked 'em up at some shelter. Most of them have clothing bins. Could be they were the only ones there. There are lots of explanations."

"Lots," Hannah said, popping the rest of the package of mints into her mouth.

Caroline decided to come right out and ask Benton. "So, Chief, I know it's too early to have say anything definitive, but as of now, do you see any connection between the murders?"

"You're right, Caroline, it's too early. Maybe I shouldn't say anything,...but I got this gut feeling..."

Ye gods, she thought, he wants me to beg him. "Yes, Chief, tell us. What do you think?" she asked.

"Well, I think it just may be Nettie Adams killed her husband and buried him under the pool house. It's just one of those funny coincidences that an intruder comes along later and kills her." Benton sat back, draping one arm over the back of his chair.

"Interesting theory, Kiel Benton", Hannah said, her eyes glinting. "A body should always respect those gut feelings. Just one thing puzzles me. If what you think is so, who hit me over the head? It was surely not the ghost of Nettie Adams!"

Caroline took Hannah aside.

"No, I do not need to go home, Carrie. I need to see Jennet. Tonight," Hannah insisted when Caroline suggested taking her straight home. "I am perfectly fine. I do not tell you what to do; you do not tell me. Agreed?"

"Okay, Granny. I just thought..."

"As the kids say: give it up, Carrie. I <u>have</u> to talk to Jennet tonight. Tomorrow is Josh's wedding and if I do not get this over with, I will not enjoy myself a bit."

The minute they let themselves quietly in Caroline's front door, Caroline realized how tired she was. Hannah, despite her ordeal, looked as if she'd had an ordinary day. The woman must be made of steel, Caroline thought. Maybe it will hit her later.

Jennet and Ian were in Caroline's living room, cozily hibernating in front of the fireplace where a roaring fire was going. Ian jumped up the moment they walked in.

"Hello! We were beginning to worry about you two," Ian said. "Oh, Caroline, before it slips my mind, I signed for a Federal Express package. It's in your study."

"Thanks, Ian," Caroline said. "Glad you're home, Jen. How are you feeling?" Jennet looked vastly improved from the last time they'd seen her. Her cheeks had some color back in them and the strained, mask-like appearance was gone. She looked like her old self. Just in time for us to drop the other shoe, Caroline thought, using one of Granny's favorite sayings.

"Much, much better. All I needed was a bit of rest. The doctor says I'm perfectly fine."

"Hope you had something to eat," Caroline said.

"We did", Jennet answered. "Ian made dinner. There is no end to this man's talents." Jennet laughed; her laugh rang delicately like wind chimes. "There's plenty left for you."

"We grabbed a pizza," Hannah said. "I am very partial to pizza, although I make a better one. Jen, if you feel up to it, we need to talk. But first, I have some bad news."

"What?" Jennet said, looking alarmed.

"Bob Adams has turned up, so to speak. I found his body this afternoon buried under Nettie's pool house. He had been dead some time, already. Probably months; maybe since he disappeared."

"Oh, I say!" Ian said.

The color drained from Jennet's face. "Hannah, that's awful. Do they think the killer is the same person who…?"

"The police are not ready to make any statement; it is too soon."

"Of course," Jennet said, some color returning to her face. "He was a dreadful man, but of course any death is tragic."

"Of course," Hannah echoed.

Caroline took Ian aside and told him about the attack on Hannah, and how she happened to find the body. "We thought there was no point in mentioning it to Jen tonight, unless she asks."

"Jennet's quite all right, Caroline. The doctor says we needn't treat her like she's ill. She took the news about that Adams fellow well. She'll find out tomorrow when she reads the paper."

"Tomorrow is Josh's wedding. You and Jennet are invited. Nobody will see a paper until evening."

"I'm looking forward to this wedding. Sounds like a jolly affair. We could use something like that to lighten our spirits," Ian said enthusiastically.

Privately Caroline thought: after Hannah asks Jennet about Aggie Wallace's allegations concerning Kaitlin, and tells her she's being blackmailed, it might take more than a wedding to lighten her spirits.

143

CHAPTER THIRTY

Sitting next to Jennet in the place Ian had vacated, Hannah decided to plunge right in. "Jennet, Carrie and I discovered Nettie was being blackmailed."

Jennet looked incredulous. "Nettie blackmailed? By whom? Over what?"

"The daughter of the woman who delivered Kaitlin."

"Oh," Jennet said, quickly. "Well, of course I remember the midwife, but I don't recall she had a daughter. Why would someone like that blackmail Nettie?" Raising nine children, Hannah had heard plenty of evasions and prevarications to know when someone was dissembling. Jennet better not try to fool Hannah. She would see right though any fib.

"Jennet, I am your friend. Anything you tell me, I will hold in confidence. You know that." Hannah reached over and took Jennet's slim hand. It was trembling.

"Oh, Hannah," Jennet said, "You know, don't you?" Jennet's lips twitched convulsively.

"Yes, Dear, I do."

"How?"

Hannah told her what Aggie had said, and what Hannah herself knew about Nettie's abnormal fear of pain.

"It seemed the perfect way out. Peter wanted a family, and Nettie had been putting him off. She didn't want to be pregnant. She was absolutely incapable of dealing with pain, or even the thought of it. It was so stupid of her; she could have been knocked out for the birth," Jennet said, her words tumbling out quickly, as if she couldn't wait to get them out. "She still wouldn't consider it. Anyhow, I had fallen in love with a man in New York…an older man… uh…" Jennet looked at her hands.

"A married man," Hannah supplied.

"Yes, although I didn't know it until I was already pregnant. He wasn't going to leave his wife. He offered to pay for an abortion, but I just couldn't do it. Yet I didn't have the courage to try to keep the child. I had a hundred reasons why not … I wasn't married, traveled all the time, it wouldn't be fair to a child, etc."

"So, Nettie offered you a perfect solution," Hannah said.

"Oh, it was, Hannah. For a while."

"What do you mean?"

"Everything went well until Nettie married Bob Adams."

"What happened then?"

"Nettie was obsessed with Bob. Nobody else counted. Then Kaitlin went away to school, and Peter won custody of her. She didn't want anything to do with her mother … I mean Nettie, or me. When our father died… Well, Hannah you know all this. Nettie and I drifted apart, and trying to maintain a relationship with Kaitlin was futile," Jennet's perfect features crumpled, making her look years older. "In a short period of time, I lost everyone I cared about."

"What are you going to do about this Wallace woman?" Hannah asked.

"Do I have a choice? If I pay her this time, she'll be back. Besides, one can hardly trust the word of such a person. What if she decides to go to Kaitlin anyway? Better she hear it from me. I'm going to have to tell Kate I'm her mother. She detests me already, what difference would it make?" Jennet asked disconsolately.

"You are right, you do have to tell her. And Jen, you must tell Peter too", Hannah said, shaking her head. He is going to be devastated, she thought. All these lies for all these years, and the truth comes out in the end. What a waste of time, of energy, of love.

"Jen, does Ian know Kaitlin is your daughter?"

Jennet shook her head. "No, but I'll tell him. If he leaves me because of it, I can't blame him. I suppose it's fit punishment," she said.

"Come on, Jennet Hope, stop feeling sorry for yourself. I have known you since your were Molly's age. You are tough. Do what has to be done and get on with your life. Forget this stuff about punishment; you have punished yourself enough."

Jennet smiled. "You're right, Hannah. I was being pretty self-indulgent."

Hannah reached over and hugged her. "You just needed a talking to by a Dutch uncle. Since one was not available, a Dutch granny had to do, already."

The following day was Josh and Susannah's wedding and Caroline agreed with Hannah that they wouldn't say anything to her family about what had happened at the Adams. Hannah didn't want anything to spoil the day. No one in the family would be likely to hear about it; they'd be too busy. Even if some of the wedding guests found out, the wedding would be over before word got around. It wouldn't be in the papers until evening and luckily, few Amish were likely to wander by a radio in someone else's house, or in town between now and then.

When Jennet and Ian arrived at the wedding, Jennet told Hannah she had called Peter and made arrangements to see him Thursday evening after the wedding was over. She hadn't been able to get in touch with Kaitlin.

By seven o'clock in the morning the wedding guests had begun to assemble. A line of Lancaster County Amish gray-topped carriages stretched for a mile down the road leading to the Schuler's home. The six teenage boys appointed to the highly coveted job as a <u>Hostler</u> or horse handler, had their hands full unhitching and stabling horses. Later they would feed the animals in shifts outside the barn since there would be too many horses to feed at the same time.

A few Mennonite and English cars, including Ian's, were among the procession. Relatives from too far away to come by carriage hired English drivers with vans, or "Amish taxis" to transport them.

Susannah, in a new lavender blue dress the color of her eyes, and Josh, dressed in a new black suit, white shirt and a black string tie, sat with two attendants each on benches inside the front door. As the guests arrived, they greeted each by name and with a handshake. The women went upstairs to leave their bonnets and coats, and the men congregated in the yard and barn.

Non-Amish guests and their Amish hosts gathered wherever they felt comfortable. Hannah and Caroline, along with Jennet, Ian and Stephen, stood on the family's glass enclosed sun porch, now filled with plants Susannah's mother was "wintering over". Most of the house had been cleared of unnecessary furniture to make room for the benches set up for the ceremony. Later, the same benches would be placed around tables and set for one of the two meals which would be served to the guests.

Ian was full of questions about the Amish ceremony, which Hannah was glad to answer. But despite her good intentions not to think about anything but the wedding today, Hannah found herself wondering if Jennet had told him about Kaitlin yet. There was no way Hannah could forget the murders either. They might be on simmer today, but she could not turn them off. Benton's suspicions about Nettie killing Bob were logical enough. She sure had the best motive. Yet, if Nettie killed her husband, why make him the beneficiary of her will? Either she was not in her right mind, or? Or what? Some thread of this was dangling just out of reach in Hannah's mind. I will let it incubate, she thought. Sooner or later it will come to me.

At eight o'clock, the male ushers or <u>Forgeher</u> called in the men from the barn. The female ushers asked the women to come down from upstairs so the ceremony could begin. The ushers were Susannah's two brothers and their wives, recently returned from an Amish settlement in South America. As Hannah explained to Ian, all the attendants at an Amish wedding were chosen by the couple as they would be in an English wedding.

The ministers were seated first, then Susannah's mother, Maria, along with Daniel and Rebecca Miller, Joshua's parents. As was usual in all Amish services, men, whether Amish or English, sat separately from women. Next came other relatives and friends.

At last, the wedding procession began. Traditionally the first to enter were any unmarried brothers and sisters of the groom. Since Caroline, as a now non-Amish person could not take part in an Amish ceremony, Bethany, Joshua's only other sibling came in alone, wearing a light blue dress with her white cap and apron. Next in the procession was a group of recently married and engaged couples. As Hannah had explained to Ian, there would be no flowers or instrumental music, only hymns. She also warned him it would be a very long ceremony, with the bride and groom leaving for ministerial instruction, before returning for the vows. She added there would be lots of a capella hymn singing in German. When the wedding had been going on about two hours, Hannah saw one of her elderly Amish neighbors, Jakey Esch, snoozing; his full beard bounced on his chest in rhythm to his snores. The others around him politely ignored his lapse.

She glanced at Ian and Stephen to see how they were faring. Both of them were awake and attentive. Finally the last words were spoken and the last hymn sung, and the wedding was officially over. There was a bustle of activity as the configuration of the room was changed. Plank trestle tables were brought in and benches rearranged. A special table, called the <u>Eck,</u> meaning corner, was set up for the immediate wedding party, so they could both see and be seen. That table would be covered with a linen cloth, decorated with the most elaborate of the seven wedding cakes, fancy dishes of nuts, fruits, candies, and be set with china dishes. The other guests would be served on unbreakable dishes which belonged to the church district and rotated among various functions as needed.

It didn't take long before the ushers showed everyone to their places. Tables, including the <u>Eck,</u> were composed of men along one side and women along the other, placement determined by age. The bridal table and surrounding tables were filled by the younger people, including Molly who had been brought by Stephen's housekeeper at the close of the ceremony.

Guests and older relatives sat at others. Hannah sat at a table with Joshua's family. She was seated next to her eldest daughter, Gwen, the wife of a bishop from another church district near Chambersburg.

Amish meals were always abundant, but a wedding feast, as in the English world, is especially bountiful. This banquet was all the more amazing considering the amount of people served in a private home. Chicken was always the main dish. Traditionally it was mixed with a bread filling. Normally there were six or seven accompanying side dishes, including mashed potatoes, creamed celery, cole slaw, fruit salad, and various vegetables. Hannah counted no less than six types of desserts, excluding the cakes. It was hard to believe anyone would want an evening meal after this, but one would be served. It would be only slightly less plenteous.

"Well, Mom," Gwen asked her in Pennsylvania Dutch, as they finished their cake. "How many quilts did you make for Joshie and Susa?"

"Chust a few." Hannah answered in English. When she spent time around the Amish speaking Pennsylvania Dutch, her normally carefully English pronunciation suffered; she reverted to a Dutch accent. "Not as many as I would like. I am slowing down already."

"Oh, sure. That would be the day," her son, Daniel answered from the head of the table. He was smiling broadly. Daniel was in a rare benign mood. It wasn't every day one's son married. After Caroline left the Amish, it had taken a long time for him to see a child married in what he considered a proper fashion - in the church. Hannah was happy for him.

Gwen turned to Hannah. "Do you know, Mom, some of those old Amish quilts, like the ones your neighbor Nettie Adams, poor thing, used to deal in, are worth up to twenty, thirty thousand dollars already?"

Hannah had a forkful of cake halfway to her mouth, and turned to look at Gwen. "<u>Gott in Himmel!mmel!</u>" Hannah said, "I know who killed Bob Adams!"

CHAPTER THIRTY ONE

Caroline had been explaining to Ian the finer points of how food is chosen for an Amish wedding, including chickens whose heads must be chopped off by the groom to be, when she saw Hannah motioning her to come outside. Caroline excused herself and followed her grandmother to the entry hall.

"Carrie, we have to go to your house a while," Hannah said, hurriedly.

"Why?" Caroline asked, knowing her grandmother must have an urgent reason for wanting to leave Josh's wedding reception.

"I chust have to look at those tapes your private investigator fellow sent from New York," Hannah said, starting up the stairs.

"Granny, can't this wait?"

"No!" Hannah said. "Go borrow Stephen's car; tell him we will be back in an hour or so already. I will get your coat," Hannah answered, on her way upstairs to the bedroom.

Caroline drew Stephen aside and asked to use his car. As the owner of the local hardware store, Stephen knew every local Amish person present and wouldn't have any problem staying at the reception all afternoon to visit. "What will I tell Ian and Jen?" he asked, as he handed Caroline his keys.

"Say Granny forgot something and I had to take her to get it. That's true enough, I suppose," Caroline answered." And, Stephen, don't let them leave until we get back."

"All right, you can explain this then," Stephen said, still looking quizzical. "But, Carrie, you aren't going near Nettie's house I hope."

"Don't worry, Fen, that's the last place I'd go," she answered.

"Okay, Granny, now tell me what this is all about," Caroline said, as she drove Stephen's Mercedes along the road.

"I need to see those tapes. I do not want to say why until you see them, too, already. I want to see if you see what I think I am going to see," Hannah said.

"You're making no sense, Gran, but I'll assume you know what you're talking about and go along with it."

"Good. Hurry," Hannah said, sitting as far forward on the seat as her seat belt would let her. She looks like she's helping drive, Caroline thought, amused.

A few minutes later, Caroline and Hannah were in Caroline's den opening a large box containing video tapes of Jennet's weekly fifteen minute syndicated television show, "Fashion Update".

Jimbo had included a letter explaining that the label on each tape showed the place and date filmed and the date shown; each was numbered and noted if it had been repeated. There were two years worth of tapes on extended play cassettes.

"Where do you want to start, Gran? At the beginning?"

"Nope," Hannah answered, picking up the remote control. "I want to start with April of this year. Show me again, how to make this thing do 'quick frozen', 'slow show' and 'giddyup'."

"That's 'freeze frame', 'pause', and 'fast forward', Gran. Here," Caroline said, trying not to laugh. She showed Hannah how to operate the remote.

"Now, Carrie, watch Jennet's face carefully, very carefully. Tell me what you see," Hannah said, leaning forward to aim the remote like a gun at the screen.

Stop, start; stop, start. For the next few minutes, they scanned the tapes.

"Now," Hannah said, stopping the machine on a close up of Jennet. An on-screen date said May 31/June 12 of the current year. "Describe what you see."

"Jen, looking ravishing in a red suit. She looks very professional and at ease. Her hair is a bit shorter than now. She's wearing about a 30" string of what looks like 8 or 9 mm. pearls - the same ones she had on today. They are either really good fakes or real, hard to tell. She has on dangling pearl earrings. That what you mean?"

"Yah," Hannah said. She advanced the tape of another date, July 22/ August 1 of this year. Another close-up of Jen filled the screen. "Now this one; again, tell me what you see."

"Let's see; there's Jen. Her hair is about the same as now. She looks a bit tired. Look at her eyes. Like she was up late - jet lag, maybe? She's wearing a green suit, looks like linen and a Hermes scarf, tied off to the side. I see the logo. That's a fancy French brand. It costs a fortune. There are the same pearls again, but different earrings - little buttons." She gazed intently at the screen. "Wait...wait! Granny! Look at the earrings! They're clip-ons! They aren't for pierced ears!" Caroline shouted, jumping up. "Granny, that's not Jennet, it's Nettie Adams!"

Hannah turned to Caroline, a confident look on her face. "Chust like I figured already; chust like I figured."

Hannah explained her conclusions to Caroline. "Part of the deal when Nettie took Jennet's baby was that the sisters would keep trading places every so often. That way, Jen was not really giving up her child, and Nettie could share in the hub-bub of Jen's career. I guess it was not too often; might cause real trouble..."

"Like Nettie could foul up Jennet's career?"

"Or Jennet could have a problem with one of Nettie's husbands. A husband might be pretty difficult to fool. How many headaches could Jennet get away with?" Hannah asked, rhetorically.

"This certainly explains a lot of the inconsistencies in how people viewed Nettie. Was it Peter or Kate who said she was like two different people? She was two different people," Caroline said. "Granny, as astonishing as this discovery is, it doesn't help us solve the murder.. Jimbo said Jennet was in New York when Nettie was killed; she has an airtight alibi."

"It is not Nettie's murder I am thinking about. I think Jennet killed Bob Adams," Hannah said.

Caroline sat on the couch with her mouth open, as frozen as the image of Nettie Adams still on pause on the TV screen.

"The date the show that is on now, shows it was filmed the day Bob Adams disappeared. That show was filmed in Paris, according to it's label. So, Nettie was thousands of miles away at the time," Hannah continued.

"We are not absolutely sure Bob was killed the day he disappeared, Granny." Caroline said.

"Where was he then? No, I think when the coroner's report comes in, it will be the same day, already. Though I know the time is not always easy to pinpoint, let us assume so for now. Believe me, Carrie, I would like nothing

151

better than to be wrong about Jennet killing Bob. But she had as much reason as Nettie if he was molesting Kaitlin, like we think."

"If Jen did it, that would explain why Nettie left Bob all her money," Caroline said. "She really did think he might come back."

"There is something else, too," Hannah said. "It's that missing thread that ties this together for me."

"What?"

"Bob Adams was wrapped in a valuable old Amish quilt. When Gwen mentioned at Josh's wedding how much those old quilts were worth these days, I knew Nettie would never waste a quilt like that, even if she was getting a body out of the house. She had dozens of others, plus regular blankets to use. And Nettie told me she gave that quilt to Jennet. I did not remember that when I saw it around Bob's remains, not until Gwen started talking about quilts. That was in July, Carrie, around the time Bob was last seen. Jen must have used it to wrap Bob's body and pull it into the pool house. It was the one quilt that would not have been missed by Nettie since she already had given it to Jen."

"I hate to keep playing devil's advocate, Gran, but there are still a couple of threads dangling. Number one: the money. Where is the $100,000 in cash Bob had? Did Jen take it? It wasn't in the pool house with the body. The police dug the whole thing up yesterday looking for evidence."

"Maybe she took it, threw it away, or hid it. Only Jennet knows that. What else?"

"Bob's car, Granny. It disappeared when he did. What happened to it? Say Jen did kill him and buried the body. Getting rid of a car is a lot harder than burying a body or even hiding money."

"I have thought of that, already," Hannah said. "Instead of taking the train like usual, say Jennet drove Bob's car back to New York and put it in storage, or in a garage she knew. She could take the train back to Lancaster and be back before Nettie arrived. Who would know? Can we trace train tickets?"

"Only if she charged it. I doubt if she'd slip up there. I can check it if you like. As for the car, there are thousands of places she could garage a car in New York, but I could have Jimbo ask around. Maybe we'd get lucky. What do you think?"

Hannah shut off the television and turned up the light. "No, that would be a waste of time. I think Jennet will crack. Despite what Ian thinks, I say she's barely holding up now. I am not going to enjoy this, Carrie, but we must know. If she did kill Bob Adams, I have to think it was not without reason."

"I hope you're right. And Nettie? We still don't know who killed Nettie, Granny."

"One thing at a time, Carrie. Besides, I have a feeling when all the facts come out about Bob's death, we will know who murdered Nettie Adams. Come on, Carrie. Let's go get Jennet. Then we are going to Nettie's house."

CHAPTER THIRTY TWO

"You go in and get her, Carrie," Hannah said, as they drove up to the Schuler house where the reception festivities were still going strong..

"What am I supposed to do, kidnap her?"

"How you do it is up to you, Carrie. Try not to be too obvious and chust do it before someone sees us lurking here, already. It looks strange for me to be coming and going. You, too. And, Carrie, don't tell Ian or Stephen where we're going. We need to have Jennet alone."

"Yes, Ma'am," Caroline said, parking the car at the side of the house as far away as she could from carriages. It wasn't unusual for guests to attend more than one wedding in a day during wedding season, so a few carriages and cars were coming and going most of the time. It made it easier for her to look inconspicuous. Even then, Granny was right. It was highly unusual for a close relative of either the bride or groom to be dashing in and out of the wedding. Caroline hoped she could be quick.

She got lucky. She found Jennet on the landing, returning from the direction of the upstairs bathroom. "Jen, Granny has found out something that will help us solve Nettie's murder, but we need your help. Can you come with us for a little while?" Caroline said.

Jennet looked somewhat surprised, but not excessively alarmed. "I suppose, but isn't this a peculiar time for all this, Caroline? Right in the middle of the reception."

"You know Amish weddings. Nothing will happen until supper; we have time," Caroline said, with a wave of her hand.

"All right, if you say so. What about Ian and Stephen?"

"I'll run and tell them; get your coat," Caroline said, heading down the stairs.

Looking into the big living room, Caroline saw Ian, with his back to her, engrossed in conversation with her father, Daniel. Stephen, standing with a group of Amishmen saw her entering and hurried over to meet her in the doorway. "Okay, Carrie, what is going on?" he asked, leading her to a secluded corner of the sun porch.

"Granny thinks she has figured out who killed Bob, but she's not ready to say until she confirms a few details. We need Jen to help us. We're going to borrow her for a while. Keep Ian here. If he asks where she is, just say she went with me and Granny. Can I keep your car for a while?"

"I don't know about this, Carrie. You aren't putting yourselves in any danger are you?"

"No, nothing like that, Fen. We'll be back by supper. Okay?"

"Why is it I think I don't have a choice?" she heard Stephen say as she headed out the door. She also heard him call, "Where are you going?" She didn't answer.

"What's this all about, Hannah?" Jennet asked as she got into the car, clutching her unbuttoned coat around her.

Caroline backed around the carriages and out onto the highway.

"We need you to put some pieces together for us, Jen dear," Hannah said, mildly.

"You're being very mysterious. I've told you everything I can think of to help solve Nettie's murder," Jennet said. She looked out the window as Caroline pulled into Nettie's drive. "Oh!" she exclaimed, realizing where she was. "Why are you bringing me here?"

"We will be here just a few minutes. Jennet, we need your help," Hannah said, soothingly.

"All right, Hannah, but this makes me very uncomfortable."

"I know; it will be fine. You must trust me," Hannah said. "Carrie, I will take Jen in through the side door. Go turn the alarm off, please."

Caroline went to the front door and deactivated the burglar alarm, then returned to let them all in through the side door to the kitchen.

They weren't in the room more than a minute or two when Jennet dropped into one of the chairs. "All right, Hannah," she said in a flat, indifferent voice. She spoke to Hannah, but looked straight ahead. "What do you want to know?"

"We want to help you, Dear, but to do that you must tell us the truth. Why did you kill Bob Adams, Jennet?"

Jennet looked emotionally rung out. Her voice, her expressions were like a zombie - devoid of any nuance of expression or emotion. "He deserved to die, but I didn't intend to kill him. He was drunk, had a gun. It was self-defense."

"Then why didn't you call the police? Why go to all the trouble of concealing the crime?"

"Because it would all come out about Kaitlin, Hannah," Jennet answered.

"You mean that she was your child?"   .

"Oh, no, not that. That Bob was sexually abusing her; and Nettie knew it all the time."

Caroline saw Hannah's intake of breath. "Oh, my," Hannah said. How do you know this?"

"Bob told me. You see, Hannah, Nettie and I traded places over the years, so I could help raise Kaitlin and she could travel to glamorous places. She didn't want me to do much about her business, preferred to leave Sadie and Annie in charge, but she loved the glamour of my job, and she was good at impersonating me, and as good at the foreign interviews as I was. I did all the hard work, preparing the interviews and coaching Nettie so she could be me." Jennet laughed, an ironic little sound. "You figured it out, didn't you?"

Hannah bobbed her head up and down.

"After she married Bob, the only times we traded was when he was out of town on a construction job. I was afraid of him; he made passes at me when I was myself; I didn't want to find out what he'd do if he thought I was Nettie. I didn't think I could plead illness like I was able to do when Nettie was married to Peter and I was taking her place." Jennet pushed her hair away from her face.

"Go on, Jen," Hannah encouraged.

"Besides, after Peter got custody of Kaitlin, I had no reason to come here and trade with Nettie. So I tried to stop the trade. Only she wasn't about to give up the glamour. She threatened to tell Kaitlin I was her mother and that kept me in line. I suppose I had a good reason to want Nettie dead, but I didn't kill her. Nor did I hire someone to kill her, if you're thinking that." Her voice sounded less flat. Some emotion was returning to Jen's recitation and her expression.

"When Nettie and I traded last summer, I knew things were bad between Nettie and Bob. He was taking more and more out-of-town jobs and Nettie suspected he was seeing someone else, someone younger. She was always jealous."

"Sounds like with some cause," Caroline said.

"Then that last time, I was here alone, thinking he was clear up in Erie, when he came home. He'd been drinking; he was not a friendly drunk, Hannah. Of course he thought I was Nettie. He told me he'd had enough of 'my' jealousy and was leaving."

"What did you say then?" Hannah asked.

"I knew it would shatter Nettie if he left, so of course, I tried to convince him to think it over. I wanted to stall him until she had a chance to talk to him. It only made him madder and madder. He screamed at me that there was someone else, someone younger. He boasted he'd cleaned out the savings account and cashed some bearer bonds. Still I kept trying to reason with him as I thought Nettie would do. I should have known better than to try to reason with him in his condition. Finally he shouted 'I' was old and said horrible obscene things about how 'I' let him sleep with...Kaitlin when 'I' couldn't satisfy him,...oh, it was awful," Jennet said, the fury of her feelings at the time suffusing her memory.

"When he said that, I just lashed out and hit him as hard as I could. That was when he pulled the gun out. He took the safety catch off. I was sure he was going to kill me, I swear it. I grabbed his arm to throw off his aim, and somehow he shot himself. The bullet went right into his chest. He was dead before I could have called anyone." Jennet shivered and wrapped her arms about herself.

"It will be all right, Jennet," Caroline said. "It was self defense. He would have killed you otherwise."

"Jen, did you drive his car back to New York and hide it?" Hannah asked.

"That's right, Hannah. I had to say he'd run away. How could I explain the car, unless he'd left by some other means. It seemed the thing to do at the time. I've been keeping it in a garage in Manhattan."

"Where are the gun and the money?"

"I hid them. After I pulled him outside on a quilt Nettie gave me, I buried him beneath the floor of the pool house and nailed the boards back in place. Then I remembered the gun and the damn money. I found the money in his car. I stuffed the gun and the money into some plumbing for the pool filter. It was the middle of the night, and I needed to go back to New York and then get back here before Nettie got home. She was flying from Paris to Harrisburg that afternoon. I thought I could come back later and get rid of the money and the gun. But I never got back. Until now." Jennet leaned forward, her head in her hands. "Oh, God", she said softly.

Caroline wasn't sure if the words were meant as a prayer or a plea.

CHAPTER THIRTY THREE

"Jen," Hannah said. "Show us where the money and the gun are hidden." Jennet raised her head from the table. "That's the easiest thing you've asked of me in several days, Hannah."

Jen looked relieved. If confession was good for the soul, it was also good for the face All the tension lines which had been there earlier, relaxed.

"Let's get this over with, Granny. I don't want to be hanging around here after dark," Caroline said. "Now I wish I had told Stephen where we were going."

"I cannot say I blame you, Carrie, for not wanting to be here," Hannah said. "I am not too keen on visiting the pool house."

Jennet looked at them oddly. Hannah remembered she'd neglected to tell Jen the circumstances under which Bob Adams' body was found, or the fact that Hannah almost joined him.

If Hannah's hunch was right, someone else knew where the body was buried. That someone was Hannah's assailant, and if Hannah's theory was right- Nettie's murderer.

159

Jennet led them out to pool house. The police had made a mess of the floor, but other than dusting for prints and a perfunctory examination, had not disturbed the plumbing area, which was off to one side. They were looking for evidence about the body and Hannah's assault, not at pipes sitting innocuously in the corner.

Jennet showed them a sturdy metal grate slightly behind the plumbing. "It's a concrete space with a drain. I was here when it was installed, so I knew about it. The cover slips right off if it's tipped." She got down on her knees, tipped the grate up and reached inside. "That's odd," she said, a puzzled expression on her face. "I don't remember reaching in very far. There was a space big enough to hide a whole briefcase of money plus the gun."

"Let me look. I have a flashlight," Hannah said, reaching into her black purse and bringing out a large sized halogen powered flashlight. She switched it on and got down for a look into the area covered by the grate. There were valves off to one side and an area of at least the size Jennet described. Other than wisps of cobwebs and dust, it was empty. "There is nothing there; it is empty."

"That can't be," Jennet said. "Let me look again." She dropped to her knees, squeezing in beside Hannah.

Caroline stooped down beside Jennet and craned her neck to see.

"Don't bother looking any more," a voice said from behind them. "You won't find anything."

Instinctively, all three women started to rise.

"Stay where you are," Sadie Shoop said, in a deadly calm voice. She stood in the doorway. Faint shafts of the setting sun came through the dusty windows of the pool house. It was enough light for Hannah to plainly see the glint of the revolver in Sadie's hand. Hannah also knew Sadie was a good shot. She'd been raised like a boy; she could hunt and fish with the best of them.

"You took the money," Jennet said.

"Why not?" Sadie asked.

"You killed Nettie, Sadie?" Jennet asked.

"No, Annie did," Hannah said. "Am I right, Sadie? So far, all you have done is <u>try</u> to kill me by hitting me over the head and putting me in with Bob Adams."

"You can be too smart for your own good, Hannah. If you had only stayed out of this..." Sadie said. "You might as well know it all now. You three won't be telling anybody.

"Annie and I were out walking the night you and Bob had that argument and you shot him, Jennet. We watched you drag him out of the house and bury him. Then we saw you hide the money and the gun."

"And you and Annie both thought Jennet was Nettie," Hannah said.

"That's right," Sadie answered. "I didn't know the truth until Jennet brought you out here now."

"Why didn't you call the police?" Caroline asked.

"Because I wanted the money. I said Bob's killer didn't deserve it, so I talked Annie into not telling. If we'd turned the killer in, the killer would tell about the money and the gun. Even if Bob's killer found the money gone later, what could she do about it?"

"But why kill Nettie?" Caroline asked.

"Annie is mentally unbalanced. Right, Sadie?" Hannah asked, shifting her weight slightly, and pressing the flashlight tightly into the folds of her dress.

"Don't say that, Hannah! Don't ever say that! Annie's not crazy, she's only high strung. She practically raised Bob Adams. How would anybody feel to see a person who was like a son killed, then carted out like a horse and thrown into a grave? No proper services, no nothing. It would be natural if an experience like that threw Annie off some."

"Off some?" Jennet shouted angrily. "She killed my sister!"

"I had to let her, had to help her," Sadie said, in a surprisingly contrite voice. "She would have done it anyway. She said justice had to be served. They would commit her, like before."

Hannah hadn't known about any commitment, but it was no surprise to her. Annie had never been "quite right." She remembered when Doc Hope tried to warn Bob Adams' mother not to let her take charge of Bob.

"And there was the money," Caroline said disparagingly. "That was part of it, too, wasn't it Sadie?"

Sadie glared at her, pointing the gun. Hannah knew time was running out. "So, Sadie," Hannah said, stalling for time while desperately hoping to think of something. "You wore some big shoes, probably weighted some clothing so you'd leave a heavier footprint as well as a bigger one, walked around in the blood and just like that, we have an intruder."

"You forgot the sighting Annie and I had of a man on our property. I thought that was a nice touch. Sent that dumb police department looking all over the cornfields," Sadie said.

"You chust thought of everything, already," Hannah said, "I have to say, pretty darn schmaert already."

A high pitched giggle came from the open doorway. "Hannah, why are you talking so Dutch?" Annie Shoop asked. She was wearing a white nightgown and was barefoot. The light slanted from the windows on the gown streaking it and her with wavering orange light.

"Annie, go home," Sadie commanded.

"No, Sadie. I can't. You promised me I could take care of Bob's killer."

161

"You did, Annie. Go home," Sadie repeated.

"No! Sadie, don't lie to me. I heard everything. But I knew it anyway. Jennet and Nettie always traded places. There is Jennet now and I'm ready..." She advanced into the room, her eyes on Jennet, her arm raised. The steel blade of a butcher knife glinted in her hand.

"Oh, God," Jennet said, as Hannah pushed Jennet down. At the same instant, Caroline dove at Annie's feet. Hannah shone the beam of the powerful flashlight directly in Sadie's face, blinding her and then threw the thing right at her midsection.

Sadie's gun discharged wildly as it clattered to the floor. Hannah grabbed it. "Carrie, are you all right?" she shouted.

"I am, Granny, but Annie's not," Caroline called back. "Annie's not moving. There's blood all over the front of her."

Sadie lay half gasping, half sobbing, the wind knocked out of her, next to her sister. Caroline was over her, the flashlight in her hand. "Give me the gun, Granny. Jen go in the house, call 911 and bring back something to tie Sadie up with."

Jennet staggered to her feet and hurried into the house.

Hannah handed the gun to Carrie. "Take this thing; I hate violence."

Later, at Caroline's house, Jen, Ian, Stephen and Hannah sat with Caroline. Benton, knowing the D.A. wouldn't press charges, declined to charge Jennet in Bob Adams' death. There would be a few formalities, but in effect the death of Annie Shoop and the arrest of Sadie closed the murder investigations.

Jen and Ian had spent some time closeted in Caroline's study while Jennet told him her story...all of it. Together they kept Jen's appointment with Peter and saw Kaitlin.

"Peter took it quite well. He knew what kind of person Nettie was," Jennet reported. "As for Kaitlin, she'll need some time, and some counseling. We'll have to see, but I think we have some basis for the right kind of relationship now."

"Well," Hannah said. "That's such good news! Almost makes up for missing the end of Josh and Susannah's wedding reception. I do enjoy a good wedding, too. I suppose they will forgive us."

"I would hope so," Ian said. "As for enjoying a good wedding, Hannah. I think I know a wedding you can attend. Very soon." He took Jennet's hand and put it to his lips.

THE END

REBECCA'S SIMPLY DELICIOUS AMISH COCONUT CAKE

(A Miller Family Tradition for Weddings)

Ingredients:

For cake:

3 Cups Sifted Cake Flour
3 teaspoons Baking Powder
1 Cup Shortening-Real Butter is Best.
2 Cups Sugar
1 teaspoon Vanilla
1 teaspoon coconut flavoring (optional)
4 Eggs, Separated
1 Cup Milk

For frosting: (Your favorite Butter-cream frosting can be substituted)

2 Cup heavy Cream
2 teaspoon Vanilla
6 Tablespoons confictioner's Sugar, sifted

2 Cups Coconut-either grated fresh or shredded from a package.

Directions:

For cake:
Sift flour, baking powder and salt together. Cream butter or shortening with sugar and vanilla until fluffy. Add beaten egg yolks and beat well. Add sifted Dry ingredients alternately with milk in small amounts, beating well after each addition. Beat egg whites until stuff but not dry and fold into batter. Pour into three nine-inch cake pans which have been oiled and floured, or oiled and lined with parchment paper. Bake in a 375 degree oven for about 25 minutes. Cool on racks for ten minutes and then turn out on wax paper cover rack to finish cooling.

For frosting:
Beat cream until stiff. Carefully add vanilla and fold in sugar. Spread between layers and over top of cooled cake layers, peaking the frosting high. Generously sprinkle with coconut.